He didn't sleep a[...] **woke for the flight home, he still hadn't put the kiss behind him. She was his best friend—they could talk about anything, right?**

He took a chance as they waited at the gate and their flight was delayed. "About last night—"

"Nothing happened last night, Param." She had used her doctor voice. "There was a lot of alcohol, you're not in a great place, I got caught up... Nothing happened." She made eye contact. "We are best friends. That's a rare thing."

He got it. They were to put the whole thing away. Chalk it up as a fluke and forget about it, to save their friendship. He nodded in agreement. His friendship with Rani was a source of sanity for him. He didn't want to lose their friendship either.

He searched her face for a moment. After what felt like an eternity, he nodded. "Agreed." He turned away from her without saying anything else.

He heard her sigh of relief and then promptly ignored the pang of pain that shot through his body. The kiss had been nothing more than a drunken fluke to Rani, and she was moving on, so he would too.

Never mind that kissing Rani had felt more right than anything else ever had.

Dear Reader,

I am beyond thrilled that you have chosen
Their Accidental Honeymoon as your next read!
Param Sheth is the groom left behind by the runaway
bride, Sangeeta Parikh, in *No Rings Attached*—and he
needs his happily-ever-after! Nothing is easily won,
even if it has been under your nose your whole life.

Param took his best friend, Rani Mistry, on his
honeymoon to get away from the viral media attention
his broken nuptials were attracting. All went well until he
kissed her on the last night.

Rani Mistry is a darn good best friend. After all, she
agreed to spend a whole week consoling brokenhearted
Param on the islands. It was a fabulous break from her
residency, until that kiss. Rani simply shuts down any
conversation about the kiss and what it might mean,
choosing to lock it up and forget about it. After all, Param
is her best friend, her rock... She can't have kisses
getting in the way—no matter how amazing!

All is well and good until Param and Rani find themselves
getting married—for real—to fulfill the requirements
of a trust that Param's grandfather left for him and his
brothers so that the money can be used to help one
of Param's brothers. As both families go excitedly into
wedding planning, Param and Rani get so caught up
in everything that they don't even realize they may be
falling in love.

I hope you enjoy reading this best-friends-to-lovers,
fake-relationship story as much as I enjoyed writing it.
Please connect with me on social media: Facebook.com/
monashroffauthor; Instagram: @monashroffauthor;
Twitter: @monashroffwrite; TikTok: @monaseesandwrites.

Happy reading!

Mona Shroff

Their Accidental Honeymoon

MONA SHROFF

HARLEQUIN

SPECIAL
EDITION

Recycling programs
for this product may
not exist in your area.

ISBN-13: 978-1-335-59448-8

Their Accidental Honeymoon

Harlequin Enterprises ULC
22 Adelaide St. West, 41st Floor
Toronto, Ontario M5H 4E3, Canada
www.Harlequin.com

Printed in U.S.A.

Mona Shroff has always been obsessed with everything romantic, so it's fitting that she writes romantic stories by night, even though she's an optometrist by day. If she's not writing, she's likely to be making melt-in-your-mouth chocolate truffles, reading, or raising a glass of her favorite gin and tonic with friends and family. She's blessed with an amazing daughter and a loving son, who have both left the nest! Mona lives in Maryland with her romance-loving husband and their rescue dog, Nala.

Books by Mona Shroff

Harlequin Special Edition

Once Upon a Wedding

The Five-Day Reunion
Matched by Masala
No Rings Attached
The Business Between Them

Visit the Author Profile page
at Harlequin.com for more titles.

To the Big Four: Anjali, Anand, Nikhil and Devika—
fall in love with your best friend
and you'll never be bored.

Acknowledgments

As always, this book is the result of a community of friends and colleagues who helped fill in the many gaps that can occur when trying to tell a story.

Huge thanks to my oldest friend, Dr. Anjali Saini, for spending hours looking up diseases and such so as to make Milan's tumor as believable as possible. (Though the "cure" that is mentioned is thoroughly fictional.)

Thank you to friend, author and agency sister Farah Heron for brainstorming this with me at our last retreat. That conversation made everything clear to me!

Huge hugs to my agent, Rachel Brooks, for her unfailing belief in me, and my editor, Susan Litman, for helping me tell a great story.

As always, special thanks to my best friend turned husband, Deven. I couldn't do this without you.

Prologue

The trouble with fancy resorts that specialized in honeymoons was that everything was geared toward happy couples. Games and drinks and activities all geared toward couples who were in love.

Rani looked up from her pink umbrella drink as the resort director, Joyce, approached them once again. Rani could have pretended to be sleeping—her sunglasses and hat provided her the ultimate hideaway—but she was here for her best friend, Param. It was her job to run interference—and pretend to be his wife.

Ugh. She really was a good friend.

She removed her sunglasses and swung her legs off the lounge chair and stood to meet Joyce before she reached Param.

Param was currently lying in the lounge chair next to her, sunglasses on, in swimming trunks and a loose

T-shirt. He took up the whole chair, his feet nearly dangling over the edge. He was pretending to sleep by the beach.

"Hey, Joyce." Rani kept her voice low as if she didn't want to wake Param.

"Hi, Rani! Just stopping by to see if you and Param were ready to join us for a Romantic Relay Race." Joyce was bubbly and sweet, but there was no way they were doing any of those couple games.

"You know, Joyce, that does sound fun, but my— Param—" she just could not say "husband" "—probably won't—"

"Actually," his deep voice came from behind her and she turned to face him, "that does sound fun."

She lowered her sunglasses and eyed him as he stood, towering over them both.

"If that's what Rani wants." He grinned at her.

Damn. She wanted whatever was going to get him out of this funk. She hadn't really expected much from him after his intended bride, Sangeeta, ran from their wedding, but the past six days of this trip had been spent with Param not really speaking as he processed. Rani gave him space, knowing he'd talk when he was ready.

Now, it seemed that with today being the last day, it seemed he was ready.

"Yes! That sounds great!" Rani gushed. "Let's do it!"

Joyce looked like Christmas had come early. "Oh yay!" she said. "Meet on the south side of the beach in five minutes!" She walked away to hunt down her next couple.

"Look at you," Rani said. "Standing up and talking and everything."

Param shook his head. "Yeah, yeah." He fell into step as they walked over to the games. "I'd say let's see how you handle it, but no one would be stupid enough to leave *you* in the mandap."

"Aw, you're making me blush." Rani rolled her eyes. "I'd never get to the mandap anyway. You know that." She bumped his shoulder. "But seriously," she stopped and he turned to face her, "Sangeeta's loss. One hundred percent."

He gave her the first smile she'd seen since his interrupted nuptials. "Come on. Let's go beat all these other couples in relay races."

"Heck yeah!" She high-fived him and they jogged over to the games.

It felt good to be moving. It felt good to laugh. And not going to lie, it felt good to win. Until Param allowed the bubbly Joyce to convince them to play The Newlywed Game, testing how well they knew each other. He and Rani had been best friends for over twenty years, so they pretty much knew everything about each other.

Except they were losing right now because they weren't a real couple. They'd never lived together. And all the questions were about daily habits. Like, sleeping habits.

"Okay." Joyce paused. "Our last question. Should be an easy one. We asked the women while the guys were gone—what side of the bed do you sleep on?"

Param froze. Never having slept in the same bed, he had no idea what side Rani slept on. Though for a split second he considered why he had never shared a bed with Rani.

He shoved the thought aside before it could take root. He'd been ready to marry another woman hardly a week ago.

He glanced at Rani and her eyes were wide. She'd had no idea how to answer this either. He shook his head. "The left?"

Joyce shook her head. "Oh no. Sorry. Rani said the right. Can't believe you missed the easiest one."

The game ended, and while they did not win, Param felt better getting away from the intimate queries. He now had a visual of Rani on the right side of the bed, with him lying next to her. He shook his head free of the image. Being left at the mandap really messed a guy up.

"Want to walk on the beach until dinner?" Param asked Rani.

"It's your show," she said. She threaded her arm through his, and they walked along the beach as the sun set.

"Thanks," he said.

"For what?"

"For coming here. For putting up with me while I pout." He shrugged.

"You know, going on prepaid island vacations is a tough thing, but I'm happy to make that sacrifice for you."

He sighed. "You know, there are a million ways to break up with someone. I have to say running from the wedding is up there as one of the worst."

"Sangeeta could have done better," Rani agreed. "But maybe it wasn't all for the worst."

"What do you mean?"

"Clearly she wasn't ready for the commitment, and maybe, she realized that you two weren't right for each other. Better before the wedding than after, don't you think?"

"Is that what happened with you and Deepak?"

Rani was silent for a moment. Then she stopped walking. They stood side by side, watching the colors of the sun as it set. She sighed deeply. "Yeah, I think so. I could not see myself spending my whole life with him, so when he proposed, I said no." She shrugged.

But Param wasn't backing off. "What was it? Like what was it that made you feel like you could not spend your life with him? Presumably, you loved him, right?"

Rani turned to him, the fading pinks and oranges of the sun radiating off her brown skin.

"Param. Sangeeta did love you. That was not a lie. But maybe you weren't The One. And I think you need to consider the possibility that maybe she wasn't The One for you either." Rani took his hand and he threaded his fingers through hers.

"Deep most definitely wasn't the one for you." Param smirked at her.

"Duh. But truthfully, I'm not looking for The One."

"Seriously?" Param raised an eyebrow. She had never wanted to talk about Deep or her other relationships before.

"Seriously. Marriage is a lot of work. There's no guarantee. Look at my sister. My dad. It can lead to devastating heartbreak." She looked out at the horizon.

"Not worth the risk." Rani said, and there was a sadness, almost wistful in nature in her voice that Param had not ever heard in the twenty plus years this woman had been his best friend.

Not true, he remembered suddenly. He had heard that in her voice when her mother had died.

"Come on." He squeezed her fingers gently. "Let's get back. We've got one dinner left and I think we need to live it up," Param said. "We'll order upstairs and watch rom-coms and thrillers all night."

"Sounds perfect!"

* * *

Room service was the best part of this place. If Rani had known that, she wouldn't have bothered dragging Param down to dinner each night.

The suite was small but luxurious. There was one bedroom and a living area, even a dining room. Param had insisted Rani take the bed, and he had taken the sofa.

When Rani emerged from the shower in shorts and a tank top, she stopped in her tracks. Param had set the food and the wine in the living area on the table in front of sofa. An old '80s rom-com—one of her favorites—was playing on the TV. As soon as he saw her, he handed her a glass of wine.

"I got you your favorite—oysters."

"What?" There was a reason he was her best friend. He always fed her well.

Param poured himself a glass and raised it to her. "To the best friend anyone ever had." He paused, trying to find the words to express himself. He had spent the week trying to make sense of what had happened, not even noticing the sun, sand or ocean. Rani had simply been there, silently supporting him. He wanted to enjoy this last night with someone who had been by his side almost his whole life. "Thank you for being here with me. Thank you for giving me space to wallow, and for helping me through all this."

"You're actually thanking me?" She smirked as she drank from her glass, motioning that he down his. "Can you afford more oysters? Because I am going to finish these."

He waved her off. "I have thanked you before."

"Ha!" she said as she sat down cross-legged on the sofa and started eating more oysters as he poured more wine for them both. She smiled, showing both her dimples. "As if."

"Fine. If I haven't, then I am right now." He handed her another glass of her favorite white wine. "Thank you."

Rani swallowed the oyster and looked him in the eye before bursting into laughter.

"What?"

"I'm your best friend. This is what we do." She sipped her wine and groaned with pleasure.

A sound Param could not recall ever hearing. He certainly would have remembered. Ugh. What was the matter with him?

"Remember when Joey Flavia dumped me in eleventh grade?"

Param sipped his wine and sat down next to her. She smelled fresh, like the fancy soap in the shower but also like sand and the ocean. Her long hair was still damp but drying in messy waves that framed her face.

"You were a mess. I must have bought twenty gallons of ice cream and a hundred boxes of tissues. And we watched rom-coms for weeks."

Rani nodded. "See?"

They finished the bottle of wine and ordered more. "I will say there is one additional thing that is regrettable about you not getting married," Rani said, clearly tipsy. "Other than not actually being married, that is."

"What's that?" He was most definitely buzzed.

She shook her head. "No. It's too mean. I won't say it."

"I'll say it." Param had been thinking it anyway. "My brothers and I all have to be married to unlock the trust that Dadaji put aside for us. And because I got stood up by my bride, we lost the money," Param said. "Why do we have to be married to get this money? Whatever. We all have jobs. We do fine. We don't need it right now anyway."

"Oh!" Rani sat straight up, or as straight up as she could considering the amount of wine she had consumed. "Listen, Milan is marrying Aisha in two months." She paused. "You'll get past this and you'll meet someone else and get married when the time is right. Then, boom, Dadaji's trust will be unlocked."

Param laughed. "You make it sound so simple."

"It is. It just doesn't feel that way right now." Rani reached out and squeezed his arm, which drove home for him how much she believed her words and wanted him to believe them, too. Rani was *not* touchy-feely. She removed her hand. "But his time, whoever she is will have to pass my test before you put a ring on it," Rani laughed and clinked glasses with him.

"Put on that thriller you like," she said.

"The one that keeps you up all night?" Param asked.

"It's fine," she insisted. "This is your show." He started to protest, but she stared him down. "Seriously."

Param put on the movie and sat back down on the sofa. Rani refilled his glass and scooted closer to him as the opening credits came on. The skin of her thighs touched his. It wasn't the first time that had happened; they'd watched countless movies together like this, but tonight, she felt like comfort. She was stability and love and that was everything he needed right now. His heart swelled with gratitude for their friendship.

"So tell me more about what happened with Deep," he prompted.

"Nothing to tell." She shrugged. "He wanted to get married. I did not. Probably wasted his time."

There was a vulnerability in her, in her words that she'd never shown him before.

Maybe it was the wine, maybe it was being dumped, he had no idea. He kissed the top of her head. "Time is never wasted with you," he whispered.

She looked up at him, as if she were about to reprimand him for that kiss, but instead, her lips fell open and he leaned toward her and brushed his lips against hers.

She didn't move away.

Then he pressed his mouth against hers and he was kissing her. She melted into him and kissed him back, and he lost the ability to think.

He pulled her close, murmured her name and rested his hands on her waist, slipping his fingers beneath her shirt to gently touch her cool skin. She deepened their kiss and the next thing he knew, he had lifted her up and she was kissing him while straddling him on the sofa…

Param's hands were warm and strong on her waist. His lips were full on her mouth, her body on top of his—what?

It was right there that sense somehow hit them both. Every muscle, every nerve in her body tensed in the same instant that he pulled his mouth away from hers.

She hastily climbed off of him and he stood.

"What the hell was that?" she asked, her brain was foggy and she was strangely cold being away from his body.

Param stared at her, wide-eyed, her confusion mirrored on his face.

"I… I don't… I'm sorry." He stepped back from her.

"We're drunk." She wrapped her arms around herself as she stood.

She could still taste him. Sweet wine and ocean.

"Yes. Yes," he gasped. "Too much wine."

"Right." She pointed a finger at him and nodded vigorous agreement. "Of course…the wine…"

"Yes. We're close…best friends, right?" He took more steps away from her. "I mean, I was about to get married—"

"Right! You're still upset. And not thinking clearly. That's what it is." She stood and walked toward the bathroom.

"Yes. That makes sense. Too much alcohol, broken heart…"

"This…" She waved a hand and frowned at the sofa and they both stared at it as if the sofa itself were to blame. "This was…nothing…just circumstances."

They locked eyes for a split second.

"We…have an early flight," Rani said.

Param nodded and retreated back toward the balcony, putting as much distance between them as possible. Like he couldn't get far enough away from her. "Yep. Early."

"I'm going to bed," she said.

"Perfect. Me too," Param agreed.

They left the food and alcohol and retreated to their respective corners.

Rani shut the door behind her. Her heart pounded in her chest. She got in bed and turned out the light. Param was her best friend, her rock. He couldn't get away from her fast enough. Made sense—he'd just been dumped. She closed her eyes and inhaled slowly to steady her heart rate. It was fine. They would go home and never talk about this. It would be like it never happened.

But forgetting his kiss would be the hardest thing she'd ever done.

* * *

Param didn't sleep a wink. He hadn't been able to get that kiss out of his head. So he took a chance and broached the subject when their flight was delayed. "About last night…"

"Nothing happened last night, Param." Rani spoke in her most clinical tone, the one she used for her patients. "There was a lot of alcohol. You're not in a great place. I got caught up…" She made eye contact. Bags under her red-rimmed eyes told him she hadn't slept well either. "You are my best friend. I treasure this relationship. Not everyone gets a friend who understands them and accepts them with all their weird faults and idiosyncrasies. It's a rare thing."

"Agreed. Too much alcohol. A lot of sharing. No need to mention it. Ever."

"Absolutely," she agreed.

"Glad we're on the same page." Chalk it up to an off night and forget about it, to save their friendship. He nodded agreement.

He heard her sigh of relief, and then promptly ignored the pang that shot through his body. The kiss had been nothing more than a drunken moment to Rani.

Never mind that kissing his best friend had felt more right than anything else ever had.

Chapter One

Eight months later

Rani walked into the warmth of her house the morning after a grueling overnight shift at the hospital. She shivered in the mudroom and stripped herself of her hat, gloves, boots and puffy winter coat.

After the long night in the peds ED, during a full moon, no less, all Rani wanted was a shower and her bed. She sniffed the air. Maybe some food first. And chai.

She walked into the mayhem that was her family. Her oldest sister, Karina, was making breakfast and bombarding their father with instructions on caring for her toddler, Veer, while she was at work. Her long, dark hair was pulled back in a French braid, and she donned chef's whites. She wasn't the tallest of the sisters, but she was taller than Papa by an inch or so. Her round face carried a mild scowl, which Rani knew hadn't been there before her divorce.

Her middle sister, Sona, was bustling around trying to get herself together for class, while chasing down Veer, who had made off with Sona's phone. Sona was the tallest of the three, having a couple inches on Karina. She looked the most like their mother—classically beautiful, high cheekbones, full lips, the whole thing—but she had their father's hazel eyes. Officially, Sona lived near the University, where she studied art after a few years of trying to find herself. But more frequently than not she spent the night at home. Their father told everyone it was because she was homesick, but Rani and Karina knew it was because there was fresh chai and homemade food at home.

Rani had been told all her life that she was the perfect blend of her parents. She had her mother's medium brown complexion, thick, wavy dark hair, and dark eyes, but she had her father's rounder bone structure.

Papa was at the stove making chai, overseeing Karina making omelets. Karina might be a control freak, but some parts of that, she came by honestly. Sachin Mistry was the omelet maker in the house, never mind that Karina was a trained chef.

The aroma of fresh chai reached Rani and instantly calmed her. Rani slipped in, grabbed a plate of eggs and a couple day-old rotli, before sitting down to inhale her food and sip her chai. It wasn't the same as her mother's. Her mother had ground her own chai spice, and Papa simply bought it. It was the one thing neither he nor Karina tried to duplicate. Even after all these years, Rani knew there was some of her mother's chai spice in the freezer. No one wanted to use it lest she truly be gone.

She grabbed a running Veer, who immediately dropped Sona's phone to hug Rani.

"How was the hospital, Rani?" Papa asked.

Karina glanced at her, just seeing her. "Hey, Rani, can you look at Veer really quick? He fell and I want to be sure he's okay."

Rani suppressed both her groan and her eye roll. If Karina could wrap Veer in bubble wrap, she probably would. Rani was her unofficial pediatrician. Karina would ask Rani's opinion, and then take Veer to the pediatrician anyway.

"Sure." Rani did a thorough check of the toddler in her arms.

"Ni Masi!" Veer gurgled his name for her as he cuddled in close. Rani melted just a little. This kid was amazing.

"He's good, Karina Ben. Nothing to worry about."

Karina whipped her braid to her back. "I'll just take him in. I already have the appointment."

Rani gritted her teeth. "Whatever. It's your money," she mumbled as Veer wiggled out of her arms to run around the kitchen some more. It's not like she was a trained pediatric emergency room doctor. Well, almost trained. Eighteen months to go.

"Veer!" Karina called out. But the little boy just giggled and continued to run. Karina turned off the stove and chased after him. Rani saw the hint of a smile on her sister's face as she chased her son.

Rani got back to her eggs. She really needed some sleep.

"Beti. Finish this. Don't waste." Her father scooped the last of the eggs into her plate. "I added extra chiles for you." He whispered as he rolled his eyes in Karina's direction.

"Thanks, Papa." Rani gratefully dug into the extra spicy.

"Rani." Sona grabbed a rotli from her plate. "Have you seen my laptop?" Sona called out.

"I've been gone for twenty-four hours. No. I have not seen your laptop," Rani snapped.

"Really? You've been gone a whole day?" Sona turned to her.

"Yes." Rani widened her eyes. "I was on shift."

"Huh. So you haven't seen my laptop?"

Rani just glared at her over her eggs.

"Hey. Jai Shri Krishna." Steve said from the door.

Rani groaned internally and shot a quick side glance at Karina, who gave Rani a small smirk while holding a wiggling Veer.

Papa met Rani's eye and they shared not rolling their eyes. Since Karina's divorce, Papa had become obsessed with getting his daughters settled, but even he could see Sona and Steve had no chemistry. Sona and Steve had been high school sweethearts, and had only recently reconnected.

"Smells amazing in here," Steve said.

"Hey," everyone chorused. It wasn't as if they didn't like Steve; she and Karina simply knew he wasn't going to be staying around. Sona was the opposite of Rani. Sona hadn't been single since she was sixteen. Rani could barely find anyone of the opposite sex that she liked well enough to spend her time with. She'd had a couple boyfriends, but inevitably, they wanted the thing she didn't have a lot to give: time.

"Hey, squirt." Steve nodded at Rani. "You've been gone a while."

Rani grinned to hide her internal grimace. He used to call her that in high school. "I'm a doctor, you know," she said as she finished her eggs.

"Fine." He rolled his eyes. "Dr. Squirt." He turned to Sona. "Your laptop is over there." He pointed to the dining room

Rani finished and stood to rinse her plate. Her bed was calling her. "I'm going to sleep." She said to anyone who might be listening.

"Rani," Papa called out. "You are meeting Ketan on Friday night."

Rani closed her eyes and inhaled, summoning all her strength. Papa seemed to have memorized her schedule, because if she had a night off, she had a date.

And they were only ever first dates, because the "men" she met were all some form of ridiculous that she couldn't tolerate in one way or another. She had asked Papa to stop with the setups, but her father could rival any matchmaking auntie and was going to see all three of his girls happily married one way or another. Rani also suspected that the fact they didn't have a mother anymore contributed to this obsession.

"Rani?" Papa required acknowledgment.

"Yep, Papa. I got it." It was only Wednesday. Papa would be reminding her for two days.

She went to her room and took a quick, hot shower. Her phone buzzed with a text from Param just as she got into bed.

I'm drowning in extra work with the school play this

semester. It's Lion King. Ms. Walter got pulled for afterschool math.

You'll make it work. You always find the time, she texted back.

Param: Mom's match-making.

Rani stared at the text from Param.

Rani: She waited eight months. I give her credit for that.

Param: You always had a soft spot for my mom.

Rani: She makes amazing dhokla.

She found herself holding her breath in anticipation of his answer. She wasn't really sure why.

Param: I'm not going on the date.

She released her breath. Of course he wasn't going. Rani had been the one to tell him that Sangeeta had run. The look on his face at that moment was not something she'd forget soon. Disbelief, betrayal and the first hints of *why am I not enough?* had crossed his almost too-handsome face.

He wasn't ready to date. Sangeeta had left him at the mandap not eight months ago. He was still grieving that relationship, not to mention his confidence and judgment were shot. Nothing could be prescribed for healing that kind of betrayal but time.

Rani: Papa set me up for Friday.

That would distract him.

Param: Again?

Rani: I have no time for this nonsense. I'm a resident. I volunteer at a clinic—and I'm never getting married.

She laughed at the eyeroll emoji Param sent, then responded, I need a nap.

She silenced her phone and lay down on her bed. Unbidden, that kiss with Param entered her consciousness. She quickly locked it up and closed her eyes. No time for mulling over a drunken mistake.

No matter how amazing it had been.

Chapter Two

Param walked into the auditorium and broke into a large smile. He knew Lion King had been a good choice. Seventh and eighth graders were familiar with the story and the characters, which made them more likely to participate. There were at least thirty children here. The most he'd had in a few years.

Seventh grade was that in-between grade that made it extra awkward in middle school. The sixth-graders were just leaving elementary school, dealing with lockers, and ever-changing class schedules. The eighth-graders were finally the big kids, strutting around the school like the pre–high schoolers they were. Param identified with being in the middle. Not as vulnerable as the young ones, not as tough as the older ones. Seventh grade was his jam.

They had assigned one of the new teachers to help

him out. Never a good sign when someone was told to do something, but he couldn't complain, he needed the extra set of hands.

He dropped his things at the base of the stage as the children chattered away. Param glanced at the clock. He'd give them ten minutes to relieve themselves of the extra energy before he got started.

"Well, you must be the famous Mr. Sheth," a woman's voice spoke from behind him.

Param turned around and found himself face-to-face with a very attractive woman. She was about Rani's height, her hair was a few shades lighter than Rani's and she had beautiful blue eyes. "I'm Mr. Sheth, but I don't know about famous."

She held out her hand. "I'm Angelina Vasquez, the new eighth-grade social studies teacher." She looked around at the mayhem, a small smile on her perfectly made-up face. "I've been assigned to help with drama club."

Param grinned and shook her hand. "Sorry about that. Ms. Walters has been doing this with me for a few years, and she got taken by the math people, so you drew the short straw. It won't be too bad, I promise. They're basically good kids."

She nodded agreement. "Just need to blow off a bit of steam at the end the day, right?" She laughed and it was tinkling sound. Param had never heard such a sound from a person. Rani's laugh was loud and hearty; she'd even been heard to snort a time or two.

He really needed to stop doing that. Comparing every woman he met to her. He did it automatically, like Rani was the ruler by which all women were measured.

"I do have some drama training. So, I'm looking forward to this."

Well, this was a pleasant surprise. Someone who actually liked drama. "Glad to hear it. We're doing Lion King, so we'll need set and costumes, and…" He looked around. "Everyone who wants a role gets a role. It's really my only rule."

She grinned at him. "I think I'm going to like working with you, Mr. Sheth."

"Call me Param."

She nodded. "Well, then, call me Angelina."

Chapter Three

Rani got off on time for once, and the clinic was closed due to lack of heat. Couldn't pay the bill was more like it. The clinic was hurting for funds, and Rani was trying to expand their pediatric "wing." She chuckled to herself. It wasn't a wing. It was one exam room that was on the opposite side of the other exam rooms, and she had commandeered it for peds.

She had found some basic pediatric equipment and gotten to work. Needless to say, the demand was greater than what she could offer, so she currently had applications out for funding and was negotiating a percentage of the donations from an upcoming fundraiser for the clinic. Neither was going to be enough to build out and make extra exam rooms, but at least she could get updated equipment. Help keep the heat on.

What she needed was a large donation or large grant,

so she could actually build out a proper wing for pediatrics. She had no shortage of doctors who were willing to volunteer their time a few times a month or more, nor was she lacking patients. She simply had nowhere to put them.

She was antsy so she decided to go to the middle school and see how the second day of Lion King was working out. When she spoke with Param yesterday, he had been excited to have an assistant teacher with a drama background.

His excitement that thirty-four students had shown up was palpable through the phone. Mostly girls. Which had made Rani chuckle. Param had no idea that at any given time, in any year, half the seventh-grade girls had a crush on him. Not that she faulted them. Param was tall and broad, with muscles all over, and he sported that classic square jaw, sensitive brown eyes and thick, wavy hair. More than that, he was soft-spoken and kind, and children picked up on genuine kindness and flocked to it. He might be her best friend, but she wasn't blind to his appeal. Growing up, more than one of her girlfriends had referred to him as "garam-garam Param." It was a play on "garam-garam," meaning hot and fresh when it came to food. Though her friends meaning was "super hot."

Watching Param naively deal with twelve- and thirteen-year-old girls with crushes was one of Rani's favorite pastimes. Though his method of dealing with it was basically to ignore the googly eyes.

She entered the school and the familiar aromas of school lunch and sweat took her back to her own awkward middle-school years. Thankfully, she and Param had had each other to navigate those treacherous years. She shook her head of the memory of mean girls.

Rani entered the auditorium where madness and mayhem ensued. Param was clearly allowing them to burn off some steam. A few of the students saw her and waved.

Rani waved back and made her way toward the stage

"Dr. Rani, this my best friend, Malini." A young girl named Amy approached her.

"Hello, Malini." Rani extended her hand. "Nice to meet you. Amy is a wonderful friend to have."

"She really is," Malini agreed. Malini had gorgeous blue eyes.

"Dr. Rani is Mr. Sheth's best friend," Amy told her friend. "But they should absolutely be going out."

Rani's eyes widened. "Excuse me?"

Amy rolled her eyes like she was sixteen as opposed to twelve. "You two are perfect together. I told Mr. Sheth yesterday when he made us write about love. He wrote about you, his best friend. I wrote about Malini because she is my best friend."

"That's great, Amy. I'll have to see what Mr. Sheth wrote about me, huh?" Rani raised an eyebrow.

"It was nice stuff. He's not mean." Amy was confident in her assessment.

She wasn't wrong. "How about you, Malini? Who did you write about?" Rani asked. Malini flushed and narrowed her eyes at Rani. "That's private."

"You are correct. Nice to meet you." The young girl was now eyeing Rani with distaste and suspicion. Oh no. Another one of Mr. Sheth's little followers.

"Nice meeting you too," Malini answered by rote. Her parents had taught her manners.

"All right, everyone." Param used a small megaphone to amplify his voice, even though Rani knew for a fact that his voice could boom loudly enough to get the children's attention. He could have used his size to intimidate, but Param would never do that. On the contrary, he went out his way to be gentle, and unintimidating. "Have a seat. We're just going to pick up where we left off."

"Mr. Sheth! Dr. Rani came to help," Trevor called out.

"I saw her. Thank you!" He turned and waved to her, a huge smile on his face. She felt instantly lighter. That's how it was with them. She waved back and took a seat and a beautiful woman who she assumed was the assistant teacher went and stood by Param.

Param had neglected to mention how gorgeous this teacher was. She had light brown skin, big blue eyes and full lips. Her dark hair was flat-iron straight and fell to the middle of her back.

"We're going to hear from Trevor for the part of Scar on the main stage. Ms. Vasquez will take anyone interested in Zazu out in the hall, and Dr. Rani will handle the hyenas in the back. As always…be respectful. No talking during auditions and certainly no unkind words or actions."

Rani stood in the back and waited for the potential hyenas to come along. She soon had a crowd of about ten. She went over a quick scene, then had the children read for the part. Twelve year olds were amazing. They weren't little children, but they weren't quite angsty teenagers either. Rani found them delightful.

Practice was amusing as she had known it would be. The hour flew by and Rani needed to leave.

Rani introduced herself to Ms. Vasquez as she was leaving.

"Oh." She smiled as shook Rani's hand. "Angelina, please. And you must be Param's best friend."

"Nice to meet you." Rani said. Angelina went back to practice.

Rani looked up at him. "Param, huh?"

"She's a colleague. I know where you're going with that face, Rani. She's pretty and kind, but she's a colleague. And I'm not ready."

He did have a panicked look about him. "Listen. Malini Sharma. She has a huge crush on Mr. Sheth."

"Rani, they're twelve."

"That's what twelve-year-old girls do. I'm just mentioning her because she has it out for me. And you know, let her down gently." Rani chuckled. "If looks could kill…"

"We're almost done here, if you need to go," Param told her.

"I do need to. I need a nap. My 'date' is tonight." Rani scowled.

Param cackled. "Come over after and tell me everything. I'll be at my parents."

Rani shook her head and rolled her eyes. "Of course."

Param finished up with the tryouts and made sure all the children were picked up before leaving school. Malini Sharma approached him a few times but each time, she flushed red and ran away.

Param treated all his kids the same way. With respect and kindness.

"She's got a little crush," Angelina said after that happened for the third time.

Param shrugged. "She'll be over it as soon as a boy her age catches her eye."

"Speaking from experience?" Angelina prodded.

He nodded. "And it's not just the twelve-year-olds." Param gathered his things and put on his coat. "All ages."

"I find that hard to believe." Angelina laughed again, that tinkling sound. Param could get used to that. He just shrugged.

"Well, it was fun. I think we have a couple Zazus," she said.

"Perfect." They walked to the parking lot. "I know tomorrow is Saturday, but we to finalize parts, so we'll all need to be here in the morning."

"I'll be there," Angelina said.

"Fantastic. See you tomorrow." Param got in his car and headed to Rani's house.

Param entered from the mudroom door on the side of the house. He'd been entering Rani's house from that door since he was ten years old. He removed his shoes, as well as all the bulky winter paraphernalia. His parents lived one street over, and he often stopped by on his way over there. Their backyards nearly bumped up to one another.

He entered the kitchen to smells of paratha being roasted with oil on the stove and dhal boiling. Karina was hard at work. In addition to her day job as a sous chef in a local chain restaurant, she also catered parties. Karina wanted to open her own restaurant, but until then, she was usually busy on Friday nights cooking for events.

"Hey! That smells amazing!" he said as he entered.

In a flash, a small bundle of energy ran toward him. "Param Mama!"

Param immediately knelt down to catch the little Tasmanian devil, before he was knocked over by Veer's enthusiastic but powerful hug. Veer quite literally threw himself into Param's arms, and Param squeezed him tight. Veer smelled like baby shampoo and sweat, and his mouth was sticky when he planted a kiss on Param's scruffy cheek. Param loved it.

"Hey, Buddy!"

"Guess what, Param Mama?" Veer beamed up at him.

"What?" Param loved that Veer referred to him as an uncle by way of being Karina's brother. It was a testament to how close their families were.

"I school today."

"What?" Param exaggerated his amazement. "You're so big!"

"I big as you." Veer laughed.

"I think so!" Param stood up, still holding Veer.

"Huh," Rani called from the steps. "I sure hope not." His best friend was forever teasing him about his height and muscles. He looked at her as he wiped whatever stickiness Veer had left on his face. She'd had a shower and put on dark jeans and a sexy little top for her date. Her hair was down, framing her face beautifully, and she'd even put on makeup.

Huh.

She looked amazing. It wasn't the first time Param has seen Rani dressed for a date, but it was the first time a pang of annoyance hit him. The top revealed a small bit of her waist and he was reminded of the silky feel of her skin when his hands had wrapped around her all those months ago. He remembered the feel of his mouth on hers—he shook his head at the memory.

Nope. Not going there.

"How did tryouts turn out? Everyone happy?" she asked, dodging Veer and his stickiness when Param put the wiggly little boy down.

"Great. Angelina is amazing! So nice to have someone around who knows what they're doing." He added a little extra excitement to his voice and gestures. Who was he?

"Fabulous!" Rani said. "I'm glad you got some proper help. I'll pop in when I can."

"She's great with the students and does not mind a little craziness. Helps when dealing with middle schoolers. Not to mention, she's very pretty." Param blurted out. What was he saying?

Rani stopped in her tracks and looked at him, a smirk on her face. "Aww. You like her."

He shrugged. "She's a colleague."

"That's how you meet people and move on." Rani said.

Rani seemed utterly undisturbed by the fact that he had said Angelina was attractive. She seemed *happy* about it.

For some reason, it annoyed him that she was undisturbed by that.

"Exactly." He said, more because he had no other answer.

Rani stopped again. "So…you're ready to move on?"

He shrugged. "I don't know. I can notice a beautiful woman, I'm not dead."

Rani shrugged. "Yeah. Okay." Her phone beeped. "I've got to go. I'll see you later at your parents?"

"Absolutely." He felt instantly lighter.

"You made more than one set of plans for tonight?" Karina asked from the stove.

"This date is hardly 'plans.' Papa is making me go." She grabbed her puffy winter coat and left.

Param watched her go, an odd pit in his stomach. He shook his head of it. She'd be at his house by nine, nine thirty at the latest. The idea calmed him.

"How's it going, Karina?" Param asked.

"Fine," she said on a sigh. He went to the counter, rolled up his shirtsleeves and started rolling out the paratha.

"When are you going to ask my sister out on a date?" Karina asked.

"Isn't Sona dating someone?" Param grinned in an effort to deflect the definite thrill of excitement that shot through him at her question. It wasn't the first time she had asked, but it was the first time she had made him flush. He ducked his face away from her.

"Not that sister, moron." Karina had taken the role of mother in this house in more ways than one.

"Rani and I are best friends. That is it," Param answered as he kept his focus on rolling paratha.

"What about this new hot teacher?"

"Karina Ben! You're worse than my mom." He made a shooing motion at her. "Go play with your child. I'll finish these."

Karina sighed and stood on her toes to try to reach Param's cheek. He had to bend down a bit. Karina kissed his cheek. "You are the sweetest. Really tall, though. And the muscles, I'm sure all the women find them entirely too big." She smirked at him. "And I saw you go all red when I asked about Rani."

"Veer!" Param called turning back to his job. "Mommy wants a big running hug!" Whatever feelings he might have about Rani were simply reactionary. Their relationship was comfortable, and they'd shared a kiss. It was normal to feel like he might want to...maybe?...date her.

It made sense, right? He still wasn't ready to take any risks, and thoughts of Rani were risk free. And they were just thoughts.

They didn't mean anything.

Did they?

Chapter Four

Rani entered from the back door of the Sheth house as she had for most of her life. She shivered in the January cold and was immensely grateful for the warmth of the mudroom when she entered. She took off her heels with a groan of relief and hung up her coat.

Param was at his parents' house for movie night. The Sheths gathered every Friday night around eight or nine for movie night. Not a mandatory thing, whoever was free would go. Param and Rani spent many a free Friday night watching movies here with both families. The moms and dads would take turns picking up the takeout and choosing the movie. Rani always remembered these nights as the best, because everyone she loved was in one room.

After her mother died, it took a bit of cajoling but the Sheth family insisted they keep up the tradition. When

Rani looked back at those days, she was ever grateful for these Friday nights, because she could count on them.

Right now, she needed to vent about her evening, and quite frankly, movie night sounded incredible. That date had robbed her of an hour of her life she would never get back.

She still had emails from the clinic head to answer, not to mention her applications for grants to help fund that clinic. If she had paid closer attention when her mother used to do this sort of work, at least she would have an idea of how to handle all of this herself. But back then Rani'd had no idea she would be following in her mother's footsteps. A movie with Param and his family felt like a balm to her soul right now.

"Hey! Is that you?" Param called from somewhere inside. She made her way to the kitchen where she knew he was. He glanced at the clock. "That didn't last long."

"I need wine," she said as a greeting. She hoisted herself up onto the island, as she had been doing for years, despite many admonitions from Auntie to not do so. It put her closer to level with Param.

He glanced at her a moment before pouring her a perfectly chilled glass. "A whole hour?"

"My dad needs to stop setting me up." She gulped at her wine.

"Spill."

"This one was the king of jerks who took me to an expensive restaurant, and then tried to order my food for me—ahi tuna salad—while he had the steak! When I tried to order my own steak, he said he wouldn't pay for it."

Param's jaw dropped, but she saw the smirk on his face anyway. "That took an hour?"

"No. I ordered the chocolate mousse on my way out and put it on his tab. I had to wait." She rolled her eyes.

Param chuckled.

"This is not funny." Rani glared at him. He was risking it right now with the laughing, considering she had a mind to do away with his entire gender.

"Where's the mousse?" Param asked, still smiling.

She sighed and produced the to-go box.

"That's what I'm talking about," Param said. He pulled out two spoons and handed her one. She waved it away in favor of her wine.

"I got two orders—for obvious reasons, and called an Uber while I waited." Rani sat down and poured more wine into her glass. She eyed the bottle. The glass was really just getting in the way.

"His setups are getting worse. Two weeks ago, a guy nearly broke a golf club after I beat him at mini golf!"

He snorted, the wine nearly coming out of his nose.

"Mini golf, Param. There were children there. He scared the shit out of them."

"Is that as bad as bringing your mom on the date?" He was leaning against the island next to her, sipping his wine and listening to her attentively. His sleeves were rolled up and Rani had to force away her gaze from his bronzed and corded forearms. He smelled amazing. A combo of the oaky cologne she had given him and spices, like he'd been cooking. Part of the reason Rani sat on the island was that it closed the height difference between her and Param. At five foot six, she wasn't exactly short, but Param towered over her and his muscles made him feel that much bigger. He was close enough to be in her space without touching her. She had the urge to scoot over closer so she was close enough to feel his heat, maybe run a finger over those forearms. She remembered those forearms holding her when she had straddled him while they kissed. She flushed and scooted away from him.

"What?" He questioned her. "Do I reek of garlic? I was helping Karina."

Rani shook her head, unable to comment. *Return to the conversation at hand.*

"At least the mom on the date was a fun person. She just didn't know how to let go of her son." Rani groaned as she recalled that nightmare. "Remember the crypto guy?" Rani shook her head as she sipped her wine again.

Param laughed again. "Yes."

He had a great laugh. *What was the matter with her?*

"You keep laughing. Your turn is coming. It's been *eight* months. Don't think your mom won't come back at you in a couple weeks," Rani warned, as she chugged her second glass and poured a third. "What I wouldn't give to not have to go on these dates anymore."

"Just tell your dad no."

"Ohh! Is that how it works? You've *met* Papa, right?" It was an understatement. Rani's father had more than once proclaimed that Param was like a son to him. "He doesn't understand 'no' if it's not what he wants to hear." She paused. "It's like he's been on a mission since Karina divorced. I mean, he's actually encouraging this thing with Sona and Steve. Even though he agrees with me and Karina that Steve may not be the guy for Sona."

"I thought you liked Steve."

"He's a nice enough guy, but do you really think he's Sona's forever guy?"

Param shrugged. "How would I know that? You're

talking to the guy whose bride left him at the mandap." He sipped his wine.

Rani rested a hand on his very hard, quite muscular shoulder. Wow. This was quite nice, touching him. "You seriously have got to stop identifying as the groom who was left behind. It's not a good look."

Param refused to meet her gaze. Even though she was on the island, he was still an imposing being. But right now, there was a bit of sadness in those deep brown eyes she knew so well. "I do not identify—"

"Param! Rani!" Aisha's panicked voice reached them from the family room. Rani jumped off the island and ran in front of Param to Aisha.

Param's younger brother, Milan was on the ground twitching. Rani knelt down immediately and laid him on his side. "Param, call 911." Her voice was naturally even and authoritative as her training came into practice.

He already had the phone to his ear.

"What happened?" Rani glanced at Aisha as she kept watch on Milan. The twitching had stopped, but his eyes were still closed.

"I…uh…we had just come back from the gym. We were chatting. We heard you two talking in the kitchen and were debating whether or not to disturb you. He was all about it, but I said you were having a private conversation, we shouldn't interrupt—"

"Aisha!" Rani had to get her back on track.

"Right." Aisha shook her head. "So all of a sudden, his eyes rolled back and he started twitching. Somehow, I caught him and was able to lay him down so he didn't hit his head. That's when I called out to you."

Rani stabilized him the best she could, ignoring

the fear that was building in her belly. She felt Param come and kneel beside her. "What can I do, Rani?" He sounded desperate, like a small child.

Rani put an arm around his broad shoulders and pulled him close to her. "We knew this could happen." She whispered in his ear, keeping her voice even and steady. "Find your parents—maybe they're in the theatre room? And call Nishant. Tell them to come to the hospital."

She could already hear the sirens in the distance. She leaned into Param with her whole body while he texted and they waited.

Rani had been the new girl at school when she met the younger two Sheth brothers. Fourth-grade politics was real, so making friends mid-year was a challenge. Rani was the most reserved of the sisters, so it was harder for her to make friends than for Sona, who was in the fifth grade, and Karina, who was in middle school.

Rani and Param were in the same class. He was already quite tall by then, but not particularly big. His hair was thick, black, and unruly. But that might have been because he kept running his long brown fingers through it. Rani had been assigned to sit next to him. She sat down and barely made eye contact. She wasn't afraid of him, but he gave off a "leave me alone" vibe that Rani understood.

A few days into the school year, Rani was at recess when a fifth-grader started picking on a smaller boy. He must have been a third-grader, but he was very thin and small, like he had been sick a lot.

The little boy did not back down from the bully,

which impressed Rani, so she watched closely. Rani herself was petite and had had her share of bully incidents. The bully was relentless, making fun of the boy's size. But it was just words, and the boy seemed unfazed.

"Can't you hear me, twerp? Where's your big brother bodyguard today? Detention, I bet. What a bunch of losers," the boy had scoffed.

"Shut up about my brother!" The little boy stood in front of this child who was twice his size. Rani closed her book and stood. The air was electric. Something was about to go down. She walked closer to where the little boy was standing. Which was when the bully stepped up his game and looked like he was about to push the little boy. But before he could, the little boy crumpled and twitched. Rani's reflexes kicked in and somehow, she caught him.

"Go get a teacher!" she screamed at whoever was around her. She lay the little boy down and watched him. He was so little, and she had no idea what was happening to him, and she was scared out of her mind.

In seconds a teacher came, and behind the teacher was the boy Rani sat next to.

"What happened to my brother?" he growled at Rani. She shook her head. "He collapsed."

Param had not looked surprised by this news.

"She caught him, Param," another kid told him.

Param looked at her, his expression softer. "Thanks. What about—"

Rani shook her head. "He didn't hit him."

The teacher had called the school nurse who called their parents and an ambulance.

It turned out that Rani's father was Milan's pediatrician, and Milas was already under the care of a neuro-

surgeon, and a pediatric oncologist. A week after his seizure, Milan had brain surgery to remove the glioma that was causing the seizures.

Her dad told the Sheth family that while Milan was fine, it was possible that the glioma might return and progress in adulthood.

After Milan's surgery, Rani wanted to visit him at the hospital. Her father cleared it with the family, and she showed up with some of her favorite books. The whole family was there, and her father introduced her.

"I just wanted to see him. And give him some books. My dad says he has to rest for a while," Rani had said.

Param stood and looked at his family. "She's the one who caught him." Param looked back at her, clear admiration on his face. "If he'd have hit his head, we might not have him right now. Thank you." Param had extended his hand.

Rani grinned and shook it. "That's what friends do."

The paramedics arrived fairly quickly. Milan was just regaining consciousness. "I'm good," he groaned. "Thanks for coming." His voice was groggy, and he had trouble sitting up, so of course, the paramedics took him in. Aisha rode with them, while Param and Rani followed in his car.

"I had just let my guard down," Param muttered as he squeezed the steering wheel.

"We all did. Milan hasn't had an incident like this since his surgery."

"The tumor. It's back, isn't it?" He glanced at her as he drove.

"There could be many reasons for having a seizure

like this. He's been on the same meds for a while—maybe they need to be changed—"

"Rani."

She took his hand and squeezed tight as if with that single gesture she could give a positive diagnosis.

"Rani." He turned to her, panic and apprehension in his eyes.

"Param." She squeezed his hand in both of hers then set it back on the steering wheel. "Let's get to the hospital."

Chapter Five

Milan had been in and out of the hospital for a bit after his surgery, and Param went with him every time. He refused to go to school and would simply leave school if his parents made him go. His parents finally gave up and let him stay with Milan during the day.

Rani would go to the hospital after school and help Param finish the schoolwork he missed, as well as his homework. She brought him books and they would read together, sitting side by side, getting lost in worlds where little brothers did not have brain surgery.

When Milan finally came home, Param remained hypervigilant over his little brother.

"I don't think you're ready to go outside and play," Param told him. They were in Milan's room at home, the walls were covered with posters of various musicians. Rani stood in the doorway, waiting.

"Mom and Dad think I am," Milan retorted as he put on his sneakers.

"Well, I'll just go check with them," Param said.

"Hey. He's fine. The doctor, who happens to be my dad, said he's fine." Rani said. "Your parents agreed. Let him play outside with us,"

"You know what? You have no idea what you're talking about. He's my little brother," Param snapped at her.

"Well, duh. But what's the point of not being in the hospital if he can't start to do regular things?" Rani shot back at him.

"You know what, Rani? Maybe you should just go home."

"Fine." Rani brushed passed him to give Milan a hug. "I'll catch up with you later." She stomped past Param on her way out without a glance.

"Fine," Param shot back as she left.

"Bhai, Rani is right. You're being nothing but a bully right now. I'm fine. What's the point of being out of the hospital if I can't have any fun?" Milan had raised his voice.

"But—"

"But nothing, Bhai. She's like your best friend and you were rotten to her." Being told off by his younger brother, Param was shocked. "I'm going outside to play. You do what you want."

Milan had opened Param's eyes, so he went to find Rani. He found her at the playground a block from their homes. "Hey."

She glared at him from the roundabout where she was spinning slowly. "Come to be a jackass to me some more?"

He couldn't help but smile. "No." He hopped on and

sat down next to her. "I came to apologize for being a jackass."

Her eyebrows shot into the air. "Milan told you off."

Even then, she had been able to see right through him. Even then, he hadn't minded one single bit. "What if he did?"

"I'm waiting."

He sighed. "I'm sorry. Really." They were barely ten years old, and had only been friends for a short time, but Param already knew she'd changed his life completely.

Her forgiveness was instant. "You know he's going to be fine."

He shook his head and tears burned behind his eyes. "No. I don't know that." He tried to stem the tears, but he failed miserably and ended up crying. After a moment, he felt Rani's arms around him. The round-about kept spinning. All she did was hold him until he was done.

Rani kept her hand on his arm while he drove them to the hospital. If she hadn't just downed half a bottle of wine, she would have driven.

Driving to the ED for work was banal—she just drove in silence to clear her head to ready herself for the shift. But driving to the ED for a loved one was fraught with nausea, racing heartbeats and fear.

When they had gotten the call that her mother had been in a car accident, she and Sona had been left at the Sheths' house. When her father had come to get her, to let her and her sisters see their mother, she hadn't wanted to go. Fear had settled into her, and she'd had no idea what to expect.

"Rani." Her mother had called to her from the hos-

pital bed. Rani stood in the doorway, leaning against her father. Her mother was propped up in the bed, a white bandage on her head, her arm and leg in casts. Rani was terrified.

"It's okay, beti. Just some broken bones." Her mother smiled. "I'm going to be fine."

She sounded fine, so Rani went to her mother. "Ma. Are you okay?"

Her mother had nodded. "Yes. I need to heal, but I'll be home before you know it."

Rani smiled, relieved. She sat next to the bed. "I was so scared."

"Me too," her mother chuckled, then coughed.

"Yeah?" Her mother wasn't afraid of anything.

"Well, yes. I was afraid I would never see you girls or Papa again." Her mother told her, as if in confidence. "And I love you so much."

"Me too."

"You love yourself?" her mother teased. It was their little joke.

Rani had rolled her eyes at her mother's comment. But she gave the appropriate answer. "Yes, I do. But I also love you so much."

They had giggled together. Rani relaxed and caught her mother up on everything that was happening.

"You know, beti, you are so very lucky to have a friend like Param, and he is equally lucky to have you." Her mother had squeezed her hands. "Treasure that."

Her mother was gone by the next morning.

They arrived in the Emergency Department shortly after the ambulance, but Nishant and his wife, Pankthi were already in the waiting room.

Param allowed Nishant to hug him while Pankthi hugged Rani. Nishant was a couple inches shorter than Param, and not quite as muscular, but they had the same hair and strong features. The way Nishant carried himself left no doubt as to who the older brother was. Pankthi was the same height as Nishant, so in heels, she was taller than him. Her hair was currently slicked back in a chic low bun, and her attire nearly matched her husband's, minus the tie. They were both lawyers in the same firm and must have rushed right over. Nishant squeezed Param's shoulder, before turning to Rani.

"What happened?" He removed his suit jacket, revealing a white dress shirt. He loosened his tie while Rani spoke.

"Param and I were in the kitchen chatting. We didn't even know Aisha and Milan were in the house until Aisha called out to us. By the time we got to him, the seizure was almost over. Param called 911 immediately and here we are."

Param ran his fingers through his hair. "Rani, can you—"

"Way ahead of you. I texted Papa. Pankthi, maybe you can find a place for everyone to sit while I poke around a bit?" Param relaxed as Rani took charge. She was amazing in a crisis.

Pankthi stood and took Nishant's hand. "You got it, Rani."

Rani put her hands on either side of Param's face. Her hands were warm and firm, her eyes had that vibrance they got when she was willing him to believe her. "This is not a crisis." She also had the weird ability of reading his mind. She continued to watch him, daring him to tell her that he just hadn't had that thought.

In times like this, he was grateful he had someone like Rani in his life. She just *knew*.

Truthfully, he was pretty much always grateful she was in his life. She was clearheaded when he wasn't, reasonable when he was irrational, not to mention she had the ability to read his mind, which rather than being disturbing was comforting.

He nodded, taking her hands in his and kissing them. Wait, what did he just do? Rani's eyes widened as his lips met her hands. That was not normal for them. At all. Yet it had felt completely normal in that second. Not to mention, putting his lips on any part of her body sent surges of …*need* through him. He felt his brother and Pankthi Bhabhi's eyes on him as well.

Just pretend it didn't happen.

Rani must have read his mind—thankfully—because she simply extracted her hands from his and stood. "I'll be back with an update." She glanced over Nishant's shoulder. "Auntie and Uncle are here." She glared at Param. *Get it together.* He nodded at her.

He watched as Rani greeted his parents before heading back into the ED.

Hugs all around as his parents came to them. Param went over what happened, pulling them into the loop. Pankthi guided them to the waiting room. "This is where Rani will come find us," she assured them.

Fifteen minutes passed with no word from Rani, but her father showed up shortly to keep them company, too.

When Rani finally arrived, her normally happy face was grim. "They're admitting him."

"They need to do some brain scans. He'd shown some growth at his last follow-up, but they want to double check, since he did have another seizure just now." Even though her job occasionally required Rani to be the bearer of not great news, she hated it more when it was someone she loved. "I pulled a string or two, and he's being admitted within the hour. Go grab a bite to eat, I'll get you his room number shortly. But no long visits. He needs to rest," Rani told them.

She met Param's eyes. He ran his hands through his hair again, so now it was all over the place. He held back with her while the family made their way to the elevator.

"Give it to me straight, Rani."

"I just did." She took his hand. "I won't lie to you."

"Rani." His voice cracked a bit on her name.

"Look at me," she ordered.

He turned to face her, fear in his brown eyes. The man was a physical mountain, but he was the biggest softie when it came to those he loved.

"Milan is the toughest of you three brothers—it's a known fact. He was the scrawny kid who stood up to bullies." She grimaced at him. "Even you."

Param let out a chuckle. "He's tough, for sure." He met her eyes and nodded. "Okay." They headed for the elevator, hand in hand. This was also new, but circumstances were odd and Param was most definitely a "physical touch" love language kind of guy. This was the third time today they'd held hands. More than their entire lives up til this point. It was not unpleasant. Their already tight connection seemed to deepen at this physical touch. Not to mention, Param seemed calmer each time.

She pushed the button and looked up at him. Most people would look at Param and expect him to be a "tough guy." They couldn't be further from the truth.

Not that Param couldn't be tough and physically intimidating when he wanted to, he just very rarely felt the need to do that. Right now, he was biting his lower lip, running his hand periodically through his hair and there was a vulnerability in his eyes that made Rani want to just hug him tight.

They joined the family in the cafeteria for coffee and hospital snacks, though Rani knew that one of her sisters was bound to show up with chai and paratha sooner or later.

The conversation was strained as no one wanted to say what was actually on their mind. Aisha played with her coffee and broke her cookie into small pieces, never really consuming anything. Rani flashed back to seeing her father do much the same thing when her mother was in the hospital.

When Rani's phone finally dinged announcing that Milan was in his room, Aisha bolted for the elevator. The rest of the Sheth family followed behind her.

The elevator doors opened to Milan's floor, and they all took their turn seeing Milan, who seemed like his normal happy-go-lucky self, except for the fact that he did not want to be in the hospital.

Param definitely relaxed some after seeing Milan looking so well, and quite frankly being a bit ornery. All normal Milan behavior.

Rani stepped away to find the neurologist. She stopped at the nurses' desk. "Who is the neuro on Milan Sheth's case?"

The older woman clicked the mouse on her computer and then looked at Rani. "It's the new guy. Dr. Kulkarni."

Rani stared at the nurse. It couldn't be. "Not Deep Kulkarni?"

The nurse checked again and nodded. "Actually, yes. Deep Kulkarni." She smiled. "You know him?"

"We went to med school together."

"So, you know." She looked at Rani over her half-eye glasses.

"Know what?"

"How devastatingly handsome he is. I'm surprised you haven't heard, even in the ED. All the young nurses are climbing over each other to work with him." The older nurse raised her eyebrows. "I'd be right there with them if I wasn't old enough to be his mother." She laughed.

"Oh, I remember," Rani said. She remembered quite well that she had not been immune to his looks and charms. Not at all.

"Well, if it isn't Rani Mistry." Speak of the handsome devil and he'll show up behind you.

The nurse widened her eyes and smirked at Rani, before Rani turned around to face her ex-boyfriend.

"Deep Kulkarni." She sing-songed. "I had no idea you were back in Maryland."

"I added neuro to my résumé, so I'm doing the residency here," he told her. Tall, dark brown skin, short-cropped hair and a smile that made women fall at his feet, Deep Kulkarni had gotten more handsome in the three years since she'd seen him. They'd been together for eight months before she broke it off. It was the longest relationship she'd ever had.

"So Milan Sheth? He's your patient?" Rani asked

"I was just going to talk to him and the family. Sheth? He's not…"

Rani grinned. "He is. Param Sheth's younger brother."

Deep inhaled. "Great. Param never liked me."

Rani laughed. "Come on. I'll protect you from big, bad Param Sheth."

They entered Milan's room and Param immediately narrowed his eyes and stood taller. Any chance of Param not recognizing Deep was out the window.

"Hello, everyone. It's good to see you all, though the circumstances are not ideal."

"Good to see you, Doc." Milan said. He side-eyed Param before continuing. "If I remember correctly, you were one of the smartest people we know—next to Rani. Glad you're on my team."

The family chorused Milan's sentiments.

"I will be the neuro on this case. I'm waiting on the MRI so we can assess if and what kind of changes we are looking at. Based on those results, we will likely need another round of testing, before seeing what our options are." He paused. "I'm sorry to throw all this at you with so little information, but I want you to be comfortable with the steps we are taking." He looked at Milan. "What questions do you have for me at this point?"

There were none. "Great." Deep nodded at the room, skimming over Param. "I'll let you know when I have some information."

"I have a gig tomorrow night," Milan said.

"I'll call them and see if they're okay with us sending Jay over. It's just a sweet sixteen," Aisha told him. Milan and Aisha were DJs and ran their own business.

"But—" started Milan.

"But nothing." His wife, his mother and Param shut him down in unison.

"We should go. Let him rest," Rani said.

Everyone said their good nights, and she and Param got back in his car.

It took him less than two seconds to ask, "So. Your ex from med school, right?"

Rani sighed. "Yeah. So?" She looked away. She did not want to talk about Deep Kulkarni right now.

Param stared at her. She felt it through her head.

"Fine. I heard through the grapevine that he moved here a while ago. I didn't cross paths with him until today." She snapped.

"I'm just saying, when you broke up, rom-coms and ice cream were not quite enough." He shook his head at her. "You were a mess."

"That is all way in the past. *I* left *him*, remember? What difference does it make if he does his job well?" Rani insisted. She *had* left him. He'd wanted more than she had been willing to give. Though Param was right— it had taken more than a few movies and gallons of ice cream to get over him.

She'd been closer to him than anyone else in her life.

Except Param. But that was a fact she'd never revealed to either man.

"It makes a difference if you're going to lose focus," Param spat at her.

"I am not losing focus." She fired up. "I *never* lost focus back then."

"Lie to yourself, but you can't lie to me," Param growled, deep in his throat, a sound she rarely heard. It was almost animal, possessive. "I was the one who helped you put your pieces back together."

Chapter Six

Param attended final tryouts the next morning as scheduled. He had tried to get out of it to go to the hospital, but his mom, Aisha, Nishant and Rani had forbidden him to do so. Tryouts turned out to be a fabulous way to distract him from sitting by Milan's bedside the way he had when they were kids. Angelina was turning out to be quite indispensable.

They wrapped up, and two of his students, Amy and Malini approached Param. "Hi, ladies. What's up?"

Amy bumped a crimson-colored Malini, but Malini said nothing. Amy finally spoke. "Malini says thanks for the opportunity to play Scar. She's very excited."

Param looked at Malini. "Congratulations. I'm sure you will be amazing."

To which Malini was able to nod before she fled. Amy shook her head and followed.

"Wow. Quite the effect you have on females." Angelina chuckled.

"Sadly, that—" he thumbed at the direction Malini ran in "—about sums it up."

"I'm sure that's not always true." They walked out to the parking lot together. "How about a coffee? Or even lunch?" Angelina asked.

"Oh." Param flushed. "Uh…normally, I'd love to. I need to get to the hospital."

"Oh." Angelina's eyes widened. "I hope everything is all right."

"Well, to be honest, I'm not sure. It's my brother. Rani says—"

"Your best friend?"

"Right. She's a doctor. Anyway, I need to get to the hospital. But how about after next practice? I know a place near the school." Whoa. He just made a date.

Angelina brightened. "Sounds great."

Param got in his car before he could do anything else out of character. Honestly, he hadn't asked anyone out since… Sangeeta. He focused on getting himself to the hospital, he didn't need time to analyze what was going on in his head. He went directly to Milan's room and found his whole family there.

"You all made me promise to go to tryouts and then you came here," Param accused.

"Yeah? So?" Nishant shrugged. "You had to work. You got it done. You're welcome."

Param narrowed his eyes at his older brother. "You don't have to work, Mr. Attorney?"

Nishant patted his bag. "Have laptop. Will travel."

"How's he doing?" Param turned to the rest of his family.

"He," Milan said loudly, "is doing just fine, considering they wake me up every two hours to poke and prod." He cut his eyes to the nurse who was doing just that at the moment.

"Best part of my job, DJ eM." She smirked.

"She's not a fan," Milan said, rolling his eyes.

"I'm a fan of DJ Ai," the nurse responded, nodding at Aisha without missing a beat. This was enough to get the family to laugh.

"Going to have to step up your game, DJ eM," Pankthi teased.

"What's so funny?" Rani asked as she entered. She was clad in scrubs and her white coat, looking very authoritative. Her presence instantly calmed Param. She wasn't a miracle worker, Param knew, but just knowing she was around, was soothing.

"The nurse is not a fan of mine," Milan reported.

"You probably complain a lot," Rani countered. She nodded at the nurse.

The nurse smiled and rolled her eyes. "Dr. Kulkarni will be by shortly." She told the room as she took her leave.

"Wait. The neurologist is stopping by?" Pankthi smirked. "The very handsome one?" She continued as she pulled out her lipstick.

"That's the one." Aisha widened her eyes and nodded. "Wow, right?"

"I'm standing right here," said Nishant.

"I'm the one in the hospital bed," Milan added.

Both women looked at their husbands and shrugged.

"You all remember Rani dated him in med school?" Param informed the group, which earned him a glare from Rani.

"No way!" Aisha and Pankthi were clearly impressed, while his brothers looked slightly nauseated.

"A few months, second year. It was really nothing." She waved a hand to dismiss it.

"We need to chat," Pankthi informed her.

Rani nodded as one of her beepers went off. "I need to take this. I'll stop by later." She pointed a finger at Milan. "Stop harassing the staff." She pointed at Pankthi and Aisha. "Be cool."

"Rani." Param laid his hand on her shoulder. "I'll walk down with you."

"Walk fast."

He fell into pace with her. "Is he going to be okay?"

"I have no test results, Param. Plus, I'm not a neurologist. Listen, Deep really is good at what he does. He'll be honest. I promise."

"It's Deep now?" Param asked.

"Seriously, what is the matter with you?" Rani asked.

"Dr. Mistry. We need you," a nurse called out.

They were down in the chaos of the ED. People in scrubs were all over the place. Medical terms were flying fast and loud. Machines beeped and burped, children cried and screamed. It was a storm, and no matter how many times Param came here, he never got used to it. But Rani, she was in her element here. "Nothing. I'm sorry. I'm just worried about Milan."

Rani hugged him quickly. "No problem."

"See you up there later?"

"Of course." She smiled as she squeezed his hand. "As soon as I can." Then she turned and calmly walked into the storm.

Chapter Seven

Deep actually came down to the ED to find Rani. "Hey, we don't usually get to see you all down here." She grinned at him as he approached.

Deep looked around at the chaos. "That's what first-year residents are for." He chuckled.

"Any news?"

Deep nodded. "The tumor is shifting and growing. That's why he's had a few seizures. We upped the meds, but that's a temporary fix." He paused and fixed his gaze on her, dark eyes intense. She'd seen him give this look to patients before. Her stomach fell into knots, she knew what he would say before he said it. "Rani, he needs to have the tumor removed."

"He's already had that done, as a child." Rani's heart was in her stomach, but outwardly she remained calm and professional.

Deep nodded. "I'm aware. In these cases, chemo is the standard of care option."

Rani was fighting to keep her professionalism. "Are there any other options?"

Deep inhaled and looked around at the chaos. He nodded toward a nearby corner that might be quieter. Rani followed. "There's a laser in Europe that has the capability needed to remove a tumor exactly like this. There has been great success in the few cases they've done. Like complete removal without harming healthy tissue." Deep hesitated. "And no recurrence. But it's still experimental. They haven't even named it yet."

"No recurrence? So you're saying he would be cured? It's a sure thing?" Rani felt hope fill inside her.

"Rani, you know there's never such a thing as a sure thing in medicine. But it may be his best shot." He paused. "You know experimental means that no insurance will cover it, and it's quite expensive."

Rani nodded. "Yes, I am aware." She inhaled. "Have you told the family?"

"I'm heading up there now. I thought you might want to join me, considering he's your best friend's brother."

Rani's mind was racing. "You know, you go on ahead. I have a few patients to clear here. I'll be there in a few. Deep, thanks so much for taking him as your patient. I really appreciate it." She squeezed his arm.

"It was nice seeing you again. I know we ended things a while ago. I kept meaning to reach out, to tell you I was in town, that I—"

"Deep." She interrupted him. No need to go down memory lane. "It's fine. You don't owe me anything." Especially since she was the one who had turned him down.

He opened his mouth like he wanted to say something. She cut him off before he started. "Thank you again, for your candor and expertise. Just don't tell the family we spoke." She started walking away.

"Of course." Deep nodded. "See you around."

Rani finished up a few patients, giving Deep enough time to talk to everyone. She knew he was done when Param texted her.

I assume you know.

I do, but I have an idea. Remember the honeymoon?

The three dots hovered for a moment then went away. Not surprising, they never talked about the honeymoon. The three dots returned with Param's response.

Which part?

All of it. On my way up. Play along.

The three dots hovered, but Rani put her phone in her pocket and pushed the elevator button for the sixth floor where Milan was. The plan was still forming in her head, but it seemed like it would work.

If Param didn't screw it up right now.

Param listened while Deep Kulkarni talked. He spoke about tumors growing and seizures returning, and long-term brain issues. Milan was twenty-eight years old. He had an entire life ahead of him. He had been lucky enough to marry his college sweetheart just a couple months ago. The two of them were currently the premier South Asian DJs around. They were booked for months.

Not to mention this was his little brother. Param had always looked out for Milan, for as long as he could remember. Maybe because Nishant had always looked after him, and Param just figured that was what big brothers did.

He had no idea what Rani's text meant. The only money was Dadaji's trust, and all three brothers had to be married for that to unlock…

Oh. No.

She wouldn't.

He closed his eyes and waited for the storm to arrive.

Rani walked into Milan's room and found Param standing beside the door, her nephew asleep on his shoulder. She smiled at him and took his hand, leaning into him. "So, did Deep—Dr. Kulkarni—stop by?" she asked the room. Both of her sisters were there to learn the results of the testing.

Auntie and Uncle were looking at her and Param with small smiles on their faces. Nishant had his eyes narrowed at them. Her father glanced at their joined hands and then drew his attention to Milan, who was answering her question.

"So, basically, he thinks this European laser thing is my best option." Milan shook his head and laughed. "He must think I have won the lottery or something. No way can I come up with that kind of cash."

"I have some saved," Nishant offered.

"Us too," Uncle said.

"I have—" Karina started.

"No. I'm not taking everyone's money. I'll apply to the charities that fund this kind of thing. I'm sure I qualify." He looked at Aisha and grinned, hopeful. "We have a bit saved as well."

Param had shifted Veer, so he could put his arm around her shoulders, pulling her into him. He was solid muscle, but he was warm and comfortable, and Rani could think of worse places to be than in Param's arms at that moment. "Are you doing what I think you're doing?" he muttered very softly into her ear.

"Just work with me," Rani muttered back. To Milan she said, "I can help you with the applications."

Milan turned to her. "That would be helpful." He ran his gaze over her and his brother and scanned the room, shaking his head. "Okay. No one else is saying anything, but as the main crisis has passed, I will ask. What the hell is going on over here?" He waved a finger between her and Param.

She flushed, and it was genuine, not fake. And when she looked at Param, he looked flushed as well. "Well," she said to him. "We should tell them."

"You can tell them," Param said.

Perfect.

"Well." Rani cleared her throat. "I don't know how much of our conversation you heard the other night, before…you know…"

"Not much. Just low murmurings," Milan said.

"Well—I mean. Well, what happened is that…" She looked at her best friend, then at the family. "Param proposed to me."

Chapter Eight

Dead silence as eight people stared at them as if they were an exhibit in a museum. Param's heart was racing, and he was desperately trying to keep a straight face. He had presence of mind enough to keep her close to him, his arm locked around her, as she leaned her head against his arm.

As if they'd stood like this before. Which they had not. He would have remembered if he had. This was a new sensation, standing this close to her, the sides of their bodies touching, his arm warm around her waist.

It was not unpleasant.

He and Rani were close—they knew each other's deepest secrets the way best friends knew things about each other. The way they were able to predict behavior, finish sentences, know each other's preferences. As close as they were, they'd never been overly touchy-feely. They'd never been physically close like this.

Except that one time.

His mind was suddenly bombarded with images and sensations he had been working to suppress. Not the least of which was the softness of Rani's skin and the strength of her legs when she had straddled him. He swallowed and returned to the present.

Rani's idea was brilliant. She was trying to get Dadaji's trust open so that Milan could have the money for this procedure. Which meant she must have talked to Deep before he came up here.

Param towered at least a head over his parents, but their scrutiny at the moment was complete and intense. His father ran his fingers through his salt-and-pepper hair, which was mostly salt, his brow furrowed. His mom's keen eyes darted from him to Rani and back. He could not tell if her reaction was happiness that was too good to be true, or suspicion.

Sachin Uncle narrowed his gaze at Rani. He was the first to speak. "I thought you were on a date with Ketan the other night."

"I…uh. Well, Papa, I was. And it was awful." Rani wasn't so smooth now.

"Why didn't you just tell me you were seeing Param?" Uncle's voice was low, but there was definitely some confusion in there.

"We were keeping it a secret." Rani took the offensive. "If I told you, you would have wanted to know when we were getting married."

Sachin Uncle opened his mouth and then shut it. "Not true."

"Well, Papa…" Karina looked at their father.

"Oh, no, Uncle, that's true…" Nishant started.

"Of course, Rani is right, Sachin," his mom said with a smile on her face. "But what does it matter?"

"It is true, old friend," his father added, clapping Sachin Uncle on the shoulder.

Uncle turned to his friend, his mouth pressed in a line, trying to suppress a smile. "Anil, you could take my side."

"Not on this one," his dad countered, a smile blooming over his features.

All eyes in the room turned to Param and Rani. Rani was still next to him, in his bubble. Veer was still sound asleep.

"What?" Rani looked at the group.

"We had hoped. All these years of friendship…but were too afraid to say anything. You two are so perfect for each other." His mother spoke with tears in her eyes. So happy.

"Mom is not wrong. It's about time!" Nishant said.

"Finally!" Sona laughed. "'Garam-garam Param' is off the market."

Milan laughed. "About time, too! Not to mention that Aisha and I won one hundred dollars from Karina and Sona. They insisted that if you two were dating, they would know. Sisters tell each other everything and all that."

"Uh-oh," Rani said for only him to hear. Her smile was unmoving, He looked at her sisters. They were eyeing her, but they broke into smiles and squealed as they came over to hug them. "I'm so happy, I don't care how much money I lost," Sona said.

Karina just shook her head. "You could have said *something*."

Rani looked up at Param and winked.

"This is truly wonderful news. All these years our families were like a family, now we really will be." His father beamed at them, happiness oozing from every part of him. A pang of regret went through Param. As if she felt that same pang, Rani looked up at him and smiled.

"Wait." His father held out his hands. "Rani said yes, right?"

She beamed and snuggled in closer to him. Her body felt amazing next to his. Why hadn't he noticed this before? Because she never snuggled into him like that before.

"Of course I did," Rani nearly squealed. Rani does not squeal. In the twenty years he had known her, she had never squealed. Not once.

"Dadaji's trust," his father said, focusing on Param. "If you two don't mind getting married sooner than later." He drew his gaze over Param's brothers. "Because as soon as you get married, the trust opens and you three will have access to that money. I'm sure there's enough in there for Milan's procedure."

"Well, if that's what you really want. We hadn't talked about it yet, but under the circumstances I'm sure we're okay with whatever. The sooner the better," Rani said. She sounded overeager. Param pressed a finger into her back as a warning. She gave a small nod and stopped herself.

Her father snapped his gaze to his daughter. "Really?"

"Yes." She spoke with more control, more logic, just like she would have if this were real. "Might as well get married as soon as possible. Especially if it might help Milan," Rani said.

"Well, we need time to plan a wedding," his mother added.

"We can keep it small and simple. At our house. Close family and friends. One hundred people max," Rani said.

"One hundred people?" His father chuckled. "Both families are hundred people easy, don't you think, Sachin?"

"Without doubt," agreed Rani's father enthusiastically.

"We need at least double that. That's the smallest we can do," his mother chimed in.

"Mom. Think about Milan," Param countered.

His mom turned to Rani. "When does Milan need the surgery?"

"According to Dr. Kulkarni, within a couple months," she answered.

"So a month," Uncle said to Param's mom as if he and Rani were not even there.

"A month?" asked Rani. Param could not tell if that was too long or too short a time.

"We'll do everything. You just show up," his mother said.

"Ooh! I'll cook," volunteered Karina.

"I will take pictures," Sona piped up.

"We will DJ," said Aisha, still holding Milan's hand.

"I will organize," said Uncle.

"Can't we just sign papers and then have a nice joint family dinner?" Rani asked. "It would be more efficient. We could have the money in a few days."

"Rani," her father nearly scolded her. "This is your wedding. Yes, we all want Milan to have the money, but a marriage should not be entered into lightly. Signing papers makes it more of a contract than a…"

"Joining of two people," finished his mother. "We will do our best to keep it simple, eh? Besides, your mother—" she looked at Uncle again and he smiled and nodded at her "—would be very angry if we let you get away with simply signing papers. You can sign the papers at the wedding."

"Not to mention, we all want to celebrate you and the big lug," Karina added.

"Honestly, we've watched you be 'friends' all these years, let us celebrate how right we were about you two," added Sona.

"Ditto," Nishant added.

"Well, it sounds like we're putting on a wedding." Milan grinned from ear to ear. "Bring it, Bhai." He raised an eyebrow at Rani. "Bhabhi."

"It seems like we're outvoted, but we insist on paying for it." Param nodded at Rani, and she nodded back.

"That's not necessary, beta," Uncle said. "We have some money saved."

"I just want us to pay and keep it simple, so whatever money there is from the trust goes to Milan," Rani said. "Besides, all we care about is being married."

Uncle did not look convinced. His mouth pressed into a line, but he did not say anything.

"Well, we can start planning tomorrow," his father said. "Tonight, we let Milan rest so he can come home tomorrow. We have many things to be grateful for."

Param felt eyes on him and turned to find Nishant watching him, his eyes narrowed.

Chapter Nine

Rani and Param exited the hospital, still hand in hand, with the rest of the family after being ousted from Milan's room to allow him to rest.

No sooner had she started the car than Param turned to her. "Have you lost your mind?"

"Listen. It was the only way I could think of to get the money for Milan," Rani insisted. "We pretend to be in… love," She quickly skirted over the word. "Get married and then after his procedure, we wait about a month and we'll get a divorce. No harm, no foul."

"Except that our families will have put on this wedding for us. And they think that we're in… love," Param had countered.

"So, let's say we secure the money, then come clean when we divorce. We'll be married for a short time, but who's going to blame us for helping Milan?" Rani insisted. "If we tell them now, they'll say it's crazy and not let us do it. Then there won't be money for Milan. Better to ask forgiveness than permission." She waved a knowing finger at him. "Even right now, had we simply gone to court and signed papers, we could get started on the money for Milan. But instead, we have an actual wedding. Besides, do you have a better idea?"

Param stared straight ahead into the night. "I do not," he conceded.

"They're going to ask how we got together," Rani warned.

"What?"

"When we watch rom-coms, do you pay attention?" Rani asked.

"Are you kidding me?" Param groaned as he lay his head back on the seat. "We're acting out one of your rom-coms?"

"*My* rom-coms? Are you serious? You make me pause every time you go for food. And rewind dialogue. I'm surprised you don't have some of it memorized."

Param lifted his head and opened his mouth as if to counter her statement, but she shot him a "oh no you don't" look, and his look turned to chagrin.

He was adorable. *What? No.*

He was flushed and chuckling at her, his dark eyes lit up in amusement. "Fine. Okay, so are you thinking like in *The Proposal* when…" He continued talking, but Rani became distracted by how his mouth moved, and how he talked with his hands and long elegant fingers. He kept talking as he pushed up his sleeves, revealing bronzed corded forearms again. Did he really not know how attractive he was? She remembered how those forearms had felt in her hands that night. She snapped her head back to the road.

Rani was no stranger to how handsome he was. "Garam-garam Param" was a play on the word "hot," as in piping hot food, but her sisters and friends applied it to him. She glanced at him as she drove. He was downright gorgeous. She might not notice it all the time, but she was noticing right now.

"What? What's that look about?"

She pressed her lips together. She had no idea what her face had just shone. She smirked. "Just glad to be the one who finally got 'garam-garam Param.'"

"I'll bet it was the honeymoon," Karina said, Veer squirming on her hip, her glass of champagne in danger of spilling over.

Aisha's eyes lit up. "I was thinking the same thing. Param was a bit off when he returned, but I thought he was getting over you-know-who."

"You can say her name. We're not in seventh grade," Rani said, sipping her champagne as she extracted herself from that conversation.

They were gathered at the Sheth house. Uncle had opened up champagne and they were celebrating Rani and Param's "engagement" as well as good news for Milan.

The family was lost in wedding planning already, saving Rani and Param from having to come up with a "how did you fall in love" story. She went back to the kitchen where Param was talking to Nishant and his father. They couldn't see her from where she was standing.

"It just sort of happened," Param was saying. "How does anyone know the minute they fell in love with their life partner?"

"Whatever," Nishant said. "I knew this was going to happen at some point."

Param shook his head. "No way you could have known that. I didn't even know that."

"Didn't you?" Nishant raised an eyebrow.

"No," Param insisted.

"What about when you were seniors in high school?" Nishant challenged.

High school? Rani leaned closer, careful not to be seen.

"I was only asking her to prom because neither of us had dates," Param answered.

"Uh-uh." Nishant shook his head. "You were *nervous*— continuously changing your prom-posal strategy." He sipped his drink.

Huh. Rani had had no idea. But then she doubted that Param knew that she had briefly crushed on him earlier that year as well. She had never acted on it— had kept her feelings to herself and locked them away. Even then, she had cherished their friendship. She had been afraid to love him even more, lest she lose him.

Losing someone you loved—a soulmate—was life-changing, devastating. She watched what had happened to her father when her mother had passed. No one knew what would happen in the future, so she was careful with who she loved.

"Whatever." Param dismissed his brother's accusations. "She asked someone on her own."

She had. She had wanted to go, so she had asked her chemistry lab partner and he had said yes. She had considered asking Param for a split second but had nixed the idea as fast as it came. Asking Param had seemed… complicated.

Param had not gone to prom. And now that she re-called it, he hadn't seemed all that thrilled to hear about it either.

"And you stayed home and watched rom-coms," Ni-shant laughed.

No way! Rani's heart melted for seventeen-year-old Param sitting home on prom night, watching rom-coms. *She knew he liked them!*

Rani leaned in farther so she could see him.

He had a beer bottle in his hand, empty champagne glass to the side. He was looking down at the bottle, peeling the label off, a small wistful smile on his face.

Rani had no idea how she knew, but she knew he was thinking about her.

That thought made her feel light and happy.

His father laughed and shook his head. "Well, none of that matters now. The point is that there is no doubt now."

"And such perfect timing," Nishant added. Rani heard the edge in Nishant's voice. He suspected some-thing. She took her glass of champagne and sauntered over to where the brothers stood.

"Hey," she threaded her arm through Param's elbow, leaning into him as she might if they were a couple, in an effort to thwart any doubt Nishant might have. She would have thought that constantly being this close to Param would feel odd, strained, but she was surpris-ingly comfortable, the closeness felt natural, exciting even. Param stiffened slightly at her touch, as if he were self-conscious, before he relaxed into her.

Param switched his gaze to her, his eyes softening, an intimate smile on his lips. "Hey yourself," he said softly.

He was a better actor than she had given him credit for. His soft voice and smile just for her ramped up her sense of closeness to him, that feeling of intimacy.

"You need to make an appointment to talk to Patel Dada. He's the lawyer in charge of that trust," Nishant told them.

They turned to look at him. Nishant would know. He was the first married and a lawyer himself. "What do you mean?" asked Param.

"I mean, there are some specific things that the third to be married has to do to unlock the trust," Nishant explained. "Make sure it's all done in such a way that the trust is available on the day you get married, so we have the money for Milan."

"Of course," Rani jumped in. "Don't want to mess that up."

Nishant grinned at her, eyes narrowed. "No, we certainly do not."

Chapter Ten

By the time Param and Rani were able to extract themselves from their families, Rani had had more wine than was completely necessary. She turned down her sister's offer to drive her home in favor of Param walking her. This was met with a chorus of "awws", that shot a bit of guilt through Param, but Rani seemed unaffected.

"I had to get away from them," Rani said as they stepped into the cold.

"What?"

"They all want to know how we got together. We have no story,"

"Fine, let's come up with one." His hands were in his pockets as they slowly walked around the long way. Silence floated between them as they each presumably were trying to come up with a suitable story.

For his part, Param was at a loss. He glanced over at Rani. She stared straight ahead, clearly lost in thought.

She didn't like for him—or anyone—to say it, but she was beautiful. He always noticed how her hair was done, whether she had on makeup or not, what she was wearing. He had no idea if all best friends noticed those things or not because he never mentioned these thoughts to anyone.

And today, holding hands, holding her body close to his—it was all more exhilarating than he would have imagined.

She sighed, turning her head to him and opening her eyes. "I do not have time to plan a wedding. The clinic is getting busier—I just got use of another exam room, but I need some muscle to clear it out."

"I hear you," he laughed. "Just tell me when and I'll come help."

"Who said I was talking about you? I got the handsome Deep Kulkarni to help." She quirked a grin at him.

He snapped his head toward her. "Ha. Good luck with that. Deep Kulkarni is not lifting a damn thing with those pretty-boy hands of his."

"Jealous?"

"Of what? If you want to go back down that road, well…" He turned to smirk at her. "I'll be here to pick up the pieces."

Rani laughed. "Ha, you are totally jealous."

"I'm not jealous. I just think you deserve someone who values you. Someone who knows what an amazing human being they have in you. Deep Kulkarni just likes how you look next to him." And she looked amazing next to Deep. But the image in his mind was of Rani next to *him*.

"You know it wasn't just that," Rani said quietly, suddenly serious.

Param shook his head. "No. You never actually said why it was over."

Rani looked straight ahead and reached for his hand. She didn't usually do this. He liked it. "It was complicated." She was silent for another moment. "He wanted to get married. We were residents so we were ridiculously busy, but we were drawn to each other. Probably, I feel, by proximity, as opposed to real emotion." She shrugged and looked down into her wine. Her voice went soft. "There is one thing I've never told anyone."

"Yeah? What's that?" Param watched her.

"I should have broken up with him sooner. I always knew that I would not marry him. I knew he was falling for me, that he wanted marriage and a family. I should have told him early on. Saved us both some grief."

This was news to Param. He had sat by her while she had cried. He had brought her coffee before her shifts. But she had never wanted to talk about the details and he had never pushed.

She shook her head, her eyes dry. "I wasn't ready. I don't think I ever will really be ready to get married. To give myself over the way you need to in that kind of relationship. It's not for me."

Param nodded. She was referring to her mother's death. Rani had never really been the same since, but then, who could be? Losing a parent at a young age could change a person. Rani, it seemed, put up walls.

"Well, his loss," Param said, bumping her shoulder. They'd bumped shoulders many times over the years, as friends do, but today was the first time he'd felt a zing. Even through their winter coats.

She was quiet, which was odd, because she always had something to say. "Huh." She spoke after a moment.

"Well, that was very nice. Apparently being engaged to you means you are nice to me." She squirmed around. "It's weird. You're almost never nice to me. I think it's making me itchy." She giggled.

That was more like it. "Don't get used to it. When do you want me to come by?"

"How about after play practice tomorrow?" Rani suggested.

"That works," Param said.

"Perfect. I just applied for funding through the hospital. I would really like to just expand the existing building, so I have multiple rooms and proper equipment. I'm sure I could get more volunteers if I had the room," Rani told him.

"Will you get it?"

"Hard to say." She sighed. "Everybody wants money. Everybody has a good cause."

"Don't worry about the wedding. The family seems more than willing to put this together. Besides, it's not for real. You can worry about planning a wedding, when it's for real."

"You're the best." She squeezed his arm and leaned into him. He snapped his head to her. She pulled back.

"Sorry." She couldn't meet his eyes. "After touching all day…"

Param shook his head and shrugged. "We didn't even talk about Milan."

"He needs that procedure." Rani turned toward him as they walked up her driveway. They must have spent hours chatting in one another's driveways. Never wanting the conversation to end. "Deep and I spoke at length about it."

"You did? When?" Why did she have to keep talking to that guy?

"He came and found me in the ED before he came to talk to you all."

"Did he?" Param smirked.

"He just wanted to give me a heads-up."

Sure he did. Jealousy sprung up in him, strong and defiant.

"The family is crazy," Rani continued. "I can't believe—"

"That they always thought we would get together?" Param chuckled.

"Yes. It's weird. We would never—" Rani stopped abruptly and he knew she was thinking about that kiss.

What part came to her mind? Was the way their mouths had fit perfectly together? Or was the instant heat between them? He knew better than to ask. Looking at her now, he could almost taste her kiss again— sweet white wine and salty oysters.

"Because we are best friends," she repeated softly.

"You're right, though." He forced himself to break her gaze. "They bought that pretty fast." He shook his head. "You sure you're okay with this?"

Rani stared at him in silence for a moment before answering. It was one of the few times he had no idea what was going through her head. "Yes." She nodded. "I'm sure. We're doing this for Milan."

"Thanks," he said softly. "You really are the best friend ever."

Chapter Eleven

Param had to miss school the next day so he could get Milan from the hospital. Everyone in the family had volunteered, but Param would not hear of it. He was going to pick up his brother and that was it. He hit the gym and showered before picking up Aisha to go with him to the hospital. The day was clear and blue, but frigid cold. He had hardly slept the night before as he tossed and turned wondering what he had gotten himself into.

Milan was packed and ready to go when they got to his room. Aisha basically bounded into her husband's arms. Milan was a few inches shorter than Param, and not nearly as muscular, and Param had always thought that Milan was the best of the brothers. Milan wrapped his arms around Aisha and kissed her like he hadn't seen her in a year, as opposed to one night.

Param cleared his throat.

"Just in case you need to see how it's done. That is how you kiss your wife." Milan grinned at a slightly dazed Aisha.

"I agree," she managed.

"Just get in the wheelchair, Lover Boy," Param told him as he rolled his eyes.

"Whatever you say, Garam-garam," Milan teased.

"Keep it up, that joke's not getting old at all," Param grumbled at his brother.

Param pushed the mandatory wheelchair into the lobby then got the car. Milan kept an ongoing diatribe the whole time. The man could talk. No wonder he was a DJ.

"I am fine with whatever you two decide," Param insisted when Milan asked about songs for the wedding. "You're the DJs."

"You don't have any special songs?" Aisha asked.

Param shook his head. They'd have to come up with something. "Well, Rani loves One Republic. Specifically, but in no particular order, 'Good Life,' 'All This Time.'" He continued to name songs. He glanced at the couple in his rearview mirror to find the two of them staring at him, their jaws down. "What?"

Milan shook his head. "Nothing." He shared a look with his wife.

"Did you write down the songs?"

"On my phone," Aisha said.

Param pulled into the driveway of Milan and Aisha's townhome and got out to open Milan's door. When he did, he found Milan staring blankly ahead, and Aisha watching him and holding his hand. He was having a small seizure. In a few seconds that felt like a year,

Milan turned to Param and then back to Aisha. "It happened again, didn't it?"

Aisha nodded, gripping his hand. "The doctor said this would happen. How do you feel?"

Milan shrugged. "A bit disoriented. But I'm good."

Param nodded and offered his hand to Milan, who waved it away. "I can get out of the car myself, Param. Don't baby me."

Param stepped back and watched Aisha and Milan walk to the front door.

"You can get my bag, though," Milan called. "Make use of those gargantuan muscles."

Param smirked at his brother's back and grabbed the bag. There would be no more tossing and turning. He and Rani would unlock that trust and get the money for Milan's surgery. That was a fact.

He dropped the bag in the house. "You two okay? Mom just texted that she wants me to go over there. Wedding stuff, I assume."

"We're good," Milan said.

"He might need a nap," Aisha said. "Then we'll work on the wedding music. Send us any more songs you want included."

"Will do," Param said. Then he hugged his brother tight, tears burning behind his eyes and prickling his nose.

"Seriously, Bhai. Check those muscles," Milan joked.

Param swallowed back the tears and pulled away. "You're just jealous because you have toothpick arms," He forced out.

"At least I don't need custom sleeves," Milan shot back.

Param laughed and the tears disappeared, just as Milan had intended. He turned his back on them and hurried to the car.

Chapter Twelve

Rani finished her shift and bundled up for the walk to the clinic. She had just worked for twenty-four hours, but the clinic was always short-staffed. Those kids needed someone to take care of them. She loved the ED. People came to her scared, tired, and she was able to assess and treat them, and make them feel better if only for a little while. She made them comfortable for the moment, she eased their pain, and hopefully calmed their panic. And she loved it.

But there were those who were forced to use the ED as a primary care clinic, because they had no access to care. She sent many of them here, to this clinic. But this facility was not equipped to see children. The children she did see were more often than not sick children in need of long-term care, not the Band-Aid that the ED offered.

She was working on expanding the clinic, but this

was a task met with more detours than seemed statistically probable. For the time being, she had turned one of the four rooms into a children's exam room. The owner of the clinic, Dr. Farah, had allowed her to make the changes she needed. But Rani's real goal was to make a pediatric clinic that could be manned by volunteer pediatricians and be the primary care for those families who needed it. Right now, she saw some of those families in her borrowed exam room.

She had secured an abandoned exam room. Now she just needed muscles to come help her empty it.

"Hi, Cami," Rani said as she entered the clinic. The young receptionist/assistant looked up from her computer.

"Hi, Doc." She smiled wide. "Great to see you. You've got three waiting."

Cami was responsible beyond her years. She kept the place running with the efficiency of a drill sergeant, which she attributed to her mother, who was in fact a drill sergeant.

Rani quickly made her way to the back where her "pediatric clinic" was located. She had missed being here at the end of last week because of that awful date. But Rani was here now, and nothing made her happier.

"I'll be right out," she said to the three families waiting for her. She dropped her bag in the small office she shared with the other doctors, hung up her coat and quickly washed her hands, before walking out to the waiting room.

She brought the first family back to the exam room. The small child was curled up in his mother's arms. "What do we have here? I'm Dr. Rani."

The mother explained that her child had had a fever

and chills for the past few days. The child certainly looked ill.

Rani gently lifted him onto the exam table and checked him out. "Mom, he has the flu. Just push fluids and rest." She grinned at the little boy. "Maybe even a popsicle." The little boy's eyes lit up. His mother thanked Rani profusely.

"I appreciate your help and having this clinic. I work two jobs and so does my husband. But we have two older children and my parents are older..." She shook her head and inhaled. "I'm not complaining. I am simply grateful that you are here." They walked out together.

"Of course," Rani said, even as her heart tugged at her. "I'm working on getting a few more rooms and another doctor or two."

The woman frowned. "You're a resident. Where will you get that kind of money? As it is, I don't know where you get the time."

Rani smiled. "I love what I do."

Patients entered nonstop for the next couple of hours. She had just walked out another patient who had the flu when Param walked in, holding a small insulated bag.

Her stomach grumbled in anticipation of whatever he had cooked. She grinned wide and waved him over. She'd just seen him yesterday, but seeing him today did all sorts happy things to her mood and interestingly— her body. She held back from hugging him. It really wasn't what they did.

They walked back to the break room and she washed up. The break room was really just a large walk-in closet that Cami had painted. Someone had brought in a small table and a couple chairs. A microwave sat on a rolling cart. Cami and her boyfriend had installed some shelves and—voilà—break room.

She and Param pulled up chairs and she dug into the bag. Dhal and rice with potato and pea shaak. Perfect. Param served them both. She practically attacked the food, she was so hungry.

"Easy there. Don't make me do the Heimlich. It's not my forte." Param joked.

He quite often cooked for her when she worked hours like this. Sometimes it was the only time they had to check in with each other.

"They decided on a heated tent," Param informed her, then hesitated. "Milan had another seizure in the car when I picked him up."

She nodded her head. "No room for doubt. This has to happen."

Param looked at her, meeting her eyes. "You really are the best." His eyes took on a glassy glow.

"I know. That's why you feed me," she jested, fanning herself.

"You know, this is the kind of thing your mom would have done," Param said. "She was always helping people, didn't care if it was out of her way," Param reflected.

She nodded. "Mom and Papa loved working together at the office. When I was like five or six, I used to get upset on the nights she worked late." Rani remembered. "One night, as I threw a minor fit, Papa loaded us into the car and took us to see her." She paused as tears burned behind her eyes. "She was volunteering at a clinic similar to this. Even then I could see how sick some of the kids were and how they lit up when they saw my mom."

"So I was right, this is exactly what your mom did."

"It's not about you being right." Rani smirked through her tears.

Param rested his hand on hers. "I know." He said softly. "How cool that you're following in her footsteps."

"Makes me feel closer to her, you know?" Rani said.

Param nodded and squeezed her hand. His hand completely engulfed hers and it made her feel safe, protected, loved.

Cami came in to get her snack as Param lay his hand on Rani's. Rani resisted the urge to pull it away when Cami passed. If they were engaged, they would hold hands like this.

"Got a new patient checking in when you get done here," Cami said, a small smile on her face.

"Thank you."

Rani quickly finished her meal and stood. "I have to get back to work."

"No problem. Go ahead. I got this," Param said.

"You're going to help clear out the other exam room?"

"Of course."

Rani washed up and headed into her one exam room. She was reading the chart as she walked in, but looked up as she heard a sharp gasp.

Her patient was Malini, from Param's class. "Well, hello." Rani beamed at her. She extended her hand to the young girl. "It's great to see you again."

Malini looked at her mother. Rani moved her hand to the mother. "Hello. I'm Dr. Mistry. I have visited Mr. Sheth's class during career day. And as I recall, Malini had some very interesting questions."

Malini's mother extended her hand to Rani. "Nice to meet you, Doctor. I'm Jessica. And I'm glad that Malini has a familiar face here."

"Of course."

"You're not going to tell anyone that I was here, are you? Mom said this was all private." Malini barked at her, but Rani noticed she was close to tears.

"No. Your mom is right. Everything here is confidential. I won't tell anyone," Rani promised.

"Even Mr. Sheth?"

"Even Mr. Sheth," Rani agreed. This seemed to make Malini feel a bit better.

"Dr. Mistry, could I have a word with you outside?" Jessica asked softly.

"Absolutely." Rani opened the door and stepped into the hallway. They took a few steps away from the room.

"I'm, uh…" Jessica looked away, her eyes glassy. "This is humiliating," She laughed sardonically. "I'm going through a nasty divorce. I lost my healthcare. It can take up to six weeks to get it back." Jessica fought back tears. "Malini is an asthmatic."

Rani touched Jessica's arm gently. "I understand. She will be well taken care of. I'm sure there's an inhaler here I can give her. Let's do the exam," Rani encouraged her.

"Thank you."

They turned to walk back into the exam room and nearly bumped into Param, who was getting ready to clear the other room. He smiled upon recognizing Mrs. Casale and opened his mouth to greet her, when Rani glared at him.

He furrowed his brow, but turned and walked the other way.

"That was my daughter's English teacher," Mrs. Casale said.

"Yes. He's my best friend," Rani said. "Let's not tell Malini he was here."

"That sounds fine." Mrs. Casale nodded. "She is already so… I think she has a crush on him."

"She absolutely does." Rani grinned.

"Well, my daughter has good taste." Mrs. Casale laughed.

"She does." Rani chuckled. "We're…well we just got engaged and we're getting married." She tested out the words on this stranger and they flowed out naturally.

"You just said he was your best friend." Mrs. Casale seemed confused.

"I did. He is. I'm marrying my best friend," Rani said. "Isn't that what they say to do? He just proposed a couple days ago." Her heart hammered in her chest and heat rushed to her face, and it wasn't because she was lying.

It was because she was telling the truth.

Chapter Thirteen

Arvind Patel was a commanding figure, his age notwithstanding. Param had grown up with Patel Dada always coming around. He and Param's grandfather had immigrated to the States together in the early 1960s, with literally the clothes on their backs and scholarships to graduate programs. They had scraped and borrowed the money for airfare and gotten off the plane with little to no idea where they were going. Both of them were taken in by a volunteer host family who met them at the airport. They lived with the Bakers for a few weeks until they saved enough money to rent an apartment of their own. The story goes that they graduated law school while working, teaching themselves how to cook along the way. Money was always lacking, so they became creative with everything.

When they had nothing and no one, they'd had each other. Their friendship deepened as their success and their families grew. It was no surprise that when Dadaji needed someone to handle the trust, he chose Patel Dada.

"Param. Rani." Patel Dada greeted them with a huge smile. "I hear congratulations are in order." He crossed his large office to hug them both.

"Thank you," Param said as he returned the hug. Dadaji hadn't been the affectionate sort of grandfather, but Patel Dada always had a hug.

"Sit. Sit." He motioned to the two empty chairs across from his desk. Patel Dada sat down behind his desk.

Patel Dada looked at Param over his half-eye glasses. "Though not the first time for you, eh?" He raised an eyebrow.

"No, Patel Dada." Param shifted uncomfortably in his seat.

"That must be awkward, with the new fiancée sitting right there next to you." He chuckled.

"Well…" Param started.

"Not really. I'm good," Rani said jovially.

Patel Dada chuckled. "Okay. Let's get to it." He placed his hands on top of a stack papers on his relatively empty desk. "Basically, you have to legitimately get married. Not just on paper, but in a ceremony. Your grandfather has not stipulated what kind of ceremony, but I'm sure your families will take care of that."

Patel Dada turned to Param, his mouth set in a line. "Your grandfather worked hard over the course of a lifetime for every cent he ever got. He paid back the loan for the tickets from India, and we have never forgotten the kindness of the Baker family."

"Of course." Param nodded.

"We worked side by side for years on very little sleep and very little food. His successes were my successes and vice versa." He shifted his hard gaze from Param to Rani and back.

They both nodded. They knew the history.

"In that light, because this is your second...attempt—" Patel Dada raised an eyebrow "—in eight months, I will be making surprise visits to check on the progress of the wedding, as well as the validity of your relationship."

"Wait. You don't believe us?" Rani sat up straight, a large amount of indignation in her voice.

"It's not that I don't believe you, so much as it's too convenient." Patel Dada's voice carried no emotion.

"Meaning?" Param sat up in his chair. Always aware that he could be a physically intimidating presence, Param generally tried to remain calm and not make sudden movements. But right now, Patel Dada was testing his ability to stay calm.

"Meaning, you need money and suddenly you two are in love and ready to get married."

"Well, we *are* in love," Rani stated firmly. "We might have waited a few extra months so our parents could have more time to plan a wedding, but you're right about one thing—Milan needs the money sooner than later. We're not so selfish that we would choose a big wedding over his well-being." Deep down she hoped he wouldn't see through her lie—except it wasn't, was it? She and Param would never make a choice like that. Family meant everything to both of them. Always had.

Patel Dada looked them over closely. "I respect your honesty. But I will not hand over your Dadaji's money until I am convinced that this is not a farce."

Param stood, his size be damned, anger boiling in him. "My brothers did not have to prove any such thing."

"True." Patel Dada nodded, his demeanor still bland.

"But even so, this situation is unique. I must remain true to your grandfather's wishes."

There was no apology in his voice. Just determination.

"What happens if the three of us never marry? What happens to the money then?" Param asked. *What if he never married? What if he never got what Nishant and Milan already had?*

Patel Dada grinned. "I am not at liberty to say."

Param shook his head. "This is ridiculous. You are literally punishing me for being left at the mandap," he barked. As if that hadn't been humiliating enough.

"I must remain true—" Patel Dada started.

"Fine." Param couldn't stand to let him finish that line again. He narrowed his eyes at the older man. "Do your 'due diligence.'" He took Rani's hand. "The only thing you will find is how much I love this woman, and how much she loves me."

Param seethed as they left the office, even as a small voice in his brain questioned why he cared so much that Patel Dada believe that he loved Rani, as opposed to believing that he simply wanted to marry her.

Chapter Fourteen

Rani held onto Param's hand until they reached his car. This was going to be harder than they'd thought. She couldn't see his eyes behind his sunglasses, but his jaw was clenched, and his body was rigid under his winter coat. Not to mention the way he was holding her hand lacked the tenderness of the night before. Instead, he held her hand with a sense of desperation. "What?"

"That man is like a second grandfather to me," Param growled. "And now he's going to check up on me to see if I'm faking a marriage for money?" His indignation was real.

"You *are* faking a marriage for money," Rani said, and Param lowered his sunglasses to glare at her. "What? It's true. You can't blame the man for being thorough. He and your grandfather worked their asses off for every dime. Side by side. Do you think he's going to just hand it over to you?"

"He could show a little faith in me. In us." Param spoke low, as if he was embarrassed that Patel Dada did not trust him. He inhaled and exhaled before turning back to her. Param shook his head and fought a grin. "I hate it when you're right."

"Sad for you that it happens all the time." Rani smirked at him as she sat down in the passenger seat.

Param put the car in gear. "It basically means we have to be convincing."

"Piece of cake." Rani snapped her fingers.

"You think so?" Param was watching the road.

"Yes. Because we already love each other."

Param shifted in his seat. Why did the word love make him fidgety every time it came up?

"How hard could it be? Our families ate it up." Rani looked out the window. She'd have more time for the clinic, not having to go on dates her father set up for her. She glanced at Param, his jaw clenched, back stiff, large hands managing the steering wheel with ease. He was offended on their behalf. She smiled to herself. Faking would be no problem, she just had to be careful not to get too used to being Param's fiancée.

"Listen, why don't I start moving some of my stuff to your place? We're going to have to live together for about a month, to make sure the money comes through. If we were really getting married, we might already be living together." They'd already be sharing a bed. She flushed and looked away from him as the image of them sharing a bed filled her mind, making her sweat, as well as reminding her of the feel of his legs beneath hers from their time on the sofa in the honeymoon suite.

Not helping her to *not* get used to being Param's fiancée.

She felt Param glance at her. She continued to stare straight ahead, her sunglasses on, lest he read the lust on her face.

Oh god, am I lusting after my best friend?

"That is true," he said, turning back to the road. "I have that extra bedroom that you crash in every so often—I made the bigger one my office."

"That's perfect. No one has to know we aren't sharing a bed." Did she say that out loud? "I mean, we are really going to be married—we simply won't have a real marriage. You'll be back to being dateless in no time."

"I'll have you know I could have a date if I wanted," Param shot back.

"Is that so?" Rani raised an eyebrow. Despite his devastating good looks and sweet personality, Param was not known for dating. He'd rather be home reading a book.

"As a matter of fact, yes. I asked out Angelina Vasquez. And she said yes."

Rani turned in her seat to face him. "You asked someone out? You kept that quiet."

"Well, we got engaged so…"

"So when are you going out?" Rani asked. She fought to keep her voice light and curious to overcome the sudden flood of what could only be jealousy that overcame her. Wow. She must really be into this whole fake marriage thing.

"Well, seeing as how I am getting married in a month…" Param bobbed his head back and forth.

"Right." Rani sat back facing front. "Try again in couple months, I'm sure she'll understand you trying to help your brother."

* * *

Param dropped her off at her house and she entered complete mayhem. Veena Auntie, Param's mom, was there. Her mom's two besties, Falguni Auntie and Simi Auntie, were also there. Not to mention Shreya Masi. And, of course, her dad's sister, Poorvi Foi. Her mother's best friends, Falguni Auntie and Simi Auntie, had been stopping by at least once a week since her mom passed, to make sure everyone was well fed. They continued this even after her father taught himself to cook. Falguni Auntie and Simi Auntie had been friends with her mom since their college days in India. They lived an hour away, but Rani felt like they were always around when her mother was alive and even after. They would reminisce and tell stories of their escapades in college. It was from listening to those conversations that Rani had learned what a strong woman her mother had been. She almost missed her mother more after hearing all those stories. But she loved hearing them anyway.

Rani knew they had reached out to her father more than once, to help him deal with his wife's death, but the truth was, he was always sadder after they had come and gone.

Her mom's sister, Shreya Masi, usually only came around when it was just them. She didn't like crowds, but here she was in the middle of the hubbub.

Papa had the whiteboard up that they used to use for Pictionary. The last time Rani had seen it was when Karina had gotten married to the Loser. On the whiteboard were labeled columns. Ganesha Puja. Mehndi. Wedding. Reception.

The four basic events of any Gujarati Hindu wedding. It looked like Papa was putting one person in charge of each function.

"Hi, Papa."

"Oh hi, beta! Listen, Veena Auntie is going to be in charge of getting your and Param's clothes together. I need you to give all of your measurements and preferences to her."

"What is going on?" Rani asked, looking around her crowded house. When was the last time this house had been filled with this much chatter and laughter? Sure, Veer did his part. But he was just one three-year-old little boy.

"We don't have a ton of time to get this wedding going, so I called in reinforcements," Veena Auntie said as she draped an arm around Rani. They were the same height. Veena Auntie's hair was cropped short and the woman had no wrinkles.

Rani looked around. Every person was busy doing something. Even her Shreya Masi was taking notes on an iPad while she chatted with one of mom's besties. And she was smiling.

"Do you remember when Deepti went paragliding? She and Sachin Bhai had a fabulous time!" Veena Auntie and Foi were reminiscing.

"How about when she did karaoke?" Falguni Auntie nearly fell off the sofa she was laughing so hard. "Your mother was a *terrible* singer." Falguni Auntie said, laughing, then caught her breath. "I was certain we would be kicked out."

Simi Auntie was wiping tears of laughter from her eyes. "Your mom would love this." She waved her hands at the commotion. "She loved a challenge, an adventure."

"Really?" asked Rani. What would her mother think

of all this? Would she see right through her farce? It might have been nice to have her here, to ask her about her confused feelings…or even to just plan her wedding.

"Oh my god. Your mom and dad hiked Kilimanjaro before Karina was born. You've seen the photos?" Falguni Auntie asked.

"Of course." Rani was always so proud of the way her mother had grabbed life.

"Your dad stopped doing all that after…" Poorvi Foi said, looking away from Rani. "I try to get him to do those things again. He used to love it. But…" She shrugged.

"Papa," Rani called out. "We could have a small simple ceremony."

"Are you joking? My youngest daughter is getting married. We need a celebration!" He said the last word with extra flare and artistic hand movements. "Especially after…everything."

By everything, he meant Karina's divorce. And Mom dying. Even though Mom had been gone fifteen years.

"Rani, beti." Poorvi Foi took her hand and pulled her close. "This is good for him. Let him do a big celebration. He needs to be excited about something, you know? You will be married regardless."

Of course, Foi was right. She hadn't seen her father like this for a long time. Not since her mother died.

She glanced at her father, his cheeks were flushed, his eyes were bright—very much how he looked when he played with Veer—and all for her wedding. She really should put an end to all the shenanigans going on in the house. The relationship may not be completely real, but as she looked around, she saw that the wedding was very real.

On impulse, she took her father's hand and guided him toward Veena Auntie. She motioned for Auntie to follow her into the den. Rani brought both of them into the room and shut the door. She needed to just be straight with them. Of course, they would be happy to go along with the plan to open the trust for Milan. Who wouldn't?

Rani closed her eyes and inhaled. When she opened them, her gaze landed on her father first. He looked confused, but there was a sparkle in his eye and a glow on his face and a sense of urgency in his stature.

She glanced at Veena Auntie, who also looked concerned but was tapping her finger while she waited for Rani to speak.

"Rani?" her father asked. "Is everything okay?"

She rested her gaze on her father. "Well…" She really should tell them the truth. But her father looked so…happy.

"Rani, you are freaking me out a bit." Papa moved closer, his brow furrowed.

Rani did not like what that furrow did to his glow. "It's just…that we just got back from Patel Dada and he's going to be doing spot-checks to make sure everything is on the up-and-up."

Her father smiled wide and pulled her into a hug. "Don't you worry one bit. Veena Auntie, Anil Uncle and I will take care of him, heh-na?" He nodded at Veena Auntie.

"You better believe it," Veena Auntie agreed.

"This is going to be the best wedding, you'll see," her father assured Rani and pulled her into a huge hug.

Veena Auntie joined in the hug. "I can't wait until you are officially my daughter too."

Rani allowed herself to be hugged and loved, all the while chastising herself for being completely gutless.

"Okay." Papa broke the hug. "Enough of all that, there's work to do."

Well, at least if Patel Dada came by here, he'd be convinced that a real wedding was happening.

Chapter Fifteen

Param dropped off Rani at her dad's, and then headed for his parents' house. Being empty nesters, his parents' home was generally organized, tidy. Tonight, Param walked in to find boxes and bags of crafting supplies everywhere. He waded through cartons of baskets and fake flowers, bags of what looked like hot glue sticks and containers of glitter. From what he saw, he was pretty sure someone had decided that their wedding colors were sage green and gray, with some maroon thrown in. He navigated the maze and found his dad in his office.

"Hey, Dad," he called. "What's going on?" he motioned to the mayhem behind him.

"Your wedding. Your mother and sisters-in-law have decided they can make decorations and favors." He shook his head and held out his hands. "I'm safer in here."

"There's no one here."

His dad's eyes lit up. "Really?" He stood. "Let's have

a beer before they come back and try to make me cut or glue something."

Param followed his father through the maze again and to kitchen, where his father handed him a cold beer.

"Hey, how did it go with Patel Dada?" His father smirked at him.

Param took a pull of his beer. "He's tough."

His father laughed. "He's a teddy bear compared to Dada."

Param shrugged, leaning against the counter. "Maybe to you, his son. But to us, Dada was a big softie." Param sighed. "Patel Dada is going to do spot-checks, make sure everything is…going smoothly."

His father sighed. "Dada missed ball games, recitals, you name it. He worked hard to get everything he had, making it easier for me to be a more hands-on father. I didn't get it as a child. But as a father, I'm oddly grateful to him." His father shrugged. "Patel Dada was the same. He's going to be careful that the money doesn't go to you boys until it's time. Even if it is for Milan. Patel Dada's loyalty is to your grandfather."

Param grinned at the memory of having his dad show up at all his school plays, and coach soccer when he was little.

"Patel Dada and your Dadaji were inseparable." He chuckled. "Dadaji once told me that he had never lived more than a block away from Patel Dada. I remember being stunned and a bit jealous. I could not fathom a friendship so deep that even as grown men they consciously made the decision to live near each other." He sighed and shook his head. "But they had it."

Funny, Param had had similar thoughts when he had moved into his own apartment. He had never been more than a five-minute walk away from Rani. Now he was a ten-minute drive. Some days it was entirely too far.

"Kind of like you and Rani," his father said as if reading his mind. His deep voice was soft and rumbly. Param had always found it soothing.

He snapped his attention back to his dad. "What?"

"You two are inseparable. Don't think I didn't know you text or talk every day. You two have a very unique connection." His father eyed him. "I have been waiting for this day for a long time."

"What day?"

"The day you finally decided to face your true feelings for Rani and marry her."

"You too, Dad?" Param sighed.

His father shook his head. "No. Don't lump me with all those people who think that a man and a woman who are best friends are bound to get together. That's not what I'm saying." He paused to finish his beer. "What I am saying, beta, is that you and Rani have always been meant to be. I've simply been waiting for you to see it."

Param stared at his father. He wasn't one for gossip or speculation or even matchmaking. His father believed what he was saying in his soul. Param shifted his weight. What exactly had his father been seeing all these years?

"So," his father was still talking, "if Patel Dada says he's coming to make sure everything is on the up-and-up, he's doing it out of love for your grandfather. No one can stand in his way."

Param sighed resignation. He and Rani were truly going to have to sell it.

Chapter Sixteen

The common chant had become, "But there's so much to do!"

Karina had already started making samples of food for them to taste, in between her shifts at the restaurant.

"Oh my god. Taste this shaak." Karina held out a spoon to Rani and Param. Rani made a motion to Param and he tasted it.

"Wow. That is amazing, Karina. Rani, taste."

Karina held out the same spoon for Rani. "Get me another spoon." Rani made a face.

Karina looked between the two of them. "Seriously, Rani? You two don't share spoons?"

"What's the big deal?" Rani reached into the drawer and got another spoon, dipped it into the shaak and tasted it. "This really is awesome."

Karina was still standing there with Param's spoon in her hand. She handed it to him, her eyes narrowing.

"I mean, you're a couple, and presumably you have swapped bodily fluids…"

Rani froze staring at her sister as the heat rushed up to her face and head. Was Karina seriously talking about swapping bodily fluids with Param standing right there? Now Rani was thinking about exchanging said fluids with her best friend—she closed her eyes and inhaled.

"What?" asked Karina as if she hadn't just dropped a bomb.

"Of course …we have…you know," jumped in Param. "Rani's just in a new stage of heightened caution because of covid and flu season. She's an emergency room doc who deals with kids. So, you know, anything to avoid bringing extra germs home." He placed his arm around her shoulders. "Right, honey?"

Honey? What the hell was *that*? She did her best to mask her face as she looked up at him. "Yes. That's it."

Karina shrugged. "Whatever. Just add it to your list of phobias, I guess."

"What do you mean?" Param still had his arm around her, but he had relaxed into her, so instead of his arm being "placed" around her, his arm was resting on her in the most natural and comfortable fashion, as if it belonged there. Rani leaned into his warmth and strength without thought. It was as if her body knew where it belonged.

"I mean that until Param here, you were a classic commitment-phobe." She shrugged. "You never dated anyone longer than a few months, at which point, you always found something wrong with them. Even that super-hot Deep Kulkarni. You never even told me he was back in town. If you weren't with Param, I'd be on you to call him."

"Hey! Fiancé. Standing right here." Param sounded reasonably irritated.

Rani smiled. Nicely done. Maybe spending all that time supervising those drama classes had served him well.

"I'm just saying that it makes sense that Rani would end up with you, though, because you are literally her longest-lasting relationship that isn't blood. She had already made a commitment to you, as a best friend. This is simply an extension of that." Karina continued on with her theory.

Rani shook her head at her sister. She had no quip because what Karina said hit close to home.

"Hey, maybe *I* should call Deep," Karina said.

"Ew! No," Rani snapped at her, at the same time that Param said, "Totally. Go for it."

Rani glared at them both. "Sister code."

Param rolled his eyes. "Did you pack up the stuff you wanted to bring to my—I mean, *our*—place?"

She looked at him. This was an entirely new and dorky side of her best friend. Honestly, it was like being in a bad '80s sitcom. He might as well have given her an exaggerated wink-wink.

"I'll go get it now."

They loaded up his car with Rani's things and drove over to Param's apartment, exchanging stories of the family's reaction to their engagement.

They unloaded and then began the process of unpacking.

"Do I really need to unpack it?" Rani sighed.

"We need to make it look good for Patel Dada," Param said as he set down the last of her boxes.

"Agreed." She looked around.

"So let's start with the rooms?" Param suggested.

They each grabbed a box and headed upstairs. Rani took her box to the small room where she crashed every so often.

"So just set that box in the hall. I'll empty this, and then—" She turned around to find that she had been talking to herself.

"Param?" She walked into the hall and met Param halfway. "Where's the other box?"

He thumbed behind him. "In my room."

She widened her eyes, but her stomach flipped. "I'm going to sleep…"

Param's turn to widen his eyes. "No!" He stepped back and put his hands in front of him. "No." He dropped his hands. "I'm just saying that some of your stuff should go in…my room, so it *looks* like you sleep in there. We won't really be sharing a bed." He was rambling.

She nodded. "Of course." She was bobbing her head ridiculously, but she was afraid if she stopped, Param would notice how flushed she was with all this talk of sharing beds and rooms. "Well, okay. Let's unpack that box." She started to walk to the room, but Param didn't move.

"Param."

"Oh yeah, right." He turned and led the way to his room.

Clearly she was not the only one disturbed by bed-sharing talk.

She'd been in his room before, many times. In fact, she had helped him move in and decorate, so there was no reason for the sweating or the butterflies in her belly as she entered his room.

She brushed past him once in the room and opened her box. The room smelled pleasantly of his bodywash and shampoo, so when she inhaled, the scent that should have calmed her, did anything but. Taking in his scent in his space was heady. She imagined what it would be like to spend the night in this room, share his bed.

"Rani? Rani!" Param repeated her name.

"Yeah. What?" She looked up at him. He had pulled some framed family photos from her box.

"Where do you want these?" He met her gaze and she was sure he could read her thoughts, but she couldn't look away.

"Just put them on my side of the bed."

His eyebrows shot up. "Your...side..." His eyes glazed over and they both stood frozen like that for just a second, but maybe it was eternity.

"Yes." Rani broke the spell, forcing a chuckle. "Couples each have a 'side of the bed.' They said so in that game we lost in the islands."

"Right." Param's turn to nod vigorously. He brushed past her and stared at the bed a second, before moving to one side. He placed the photo on the end table and turned to her. "Your side."

"Perfect." She said, returning to the box, desperate to not imagine herself actually sleeping right there next to him.

She failed.

Chapter Seventeen

They ended up taking two cars on a three-hour pilgrim-
age to Edison because Veena Auntie, who, as a seamstress,
was the natural choice to pick out their clothes, insisted
that it was the only place to go for wedding clothes.

"Trust me," she told Rani. "Your mom would agree."

Rani nodded her agreement, knowing that her mother
and Auntie had been quite close.

Without warning, tears burned at her eyes. She was
getting married without her mother. Param wrapped
his arm around her—she was getting used to this—and
pulled her close, his mouth near her ear as he whispered
to her. "It'll be okay."

She allowed herself to melt into his comfort.

*"Mom. You were a beautiful bride." Rani was look-
ing at a wedding portrait of her parents that her mother
had just gotten around to hanging.*

"Thank you, beti." Her mother had squeezed her tight. "Every bride is beautiful." She had looked down at her daughter. "It shows when you are in love."

"Really?" Fifteen-year-old Rani was skeptical. "It looked like makeup and jewelry were doing the trick."

"Of course," her mother had said. "Makeup and jewelry are fine, but they can only do so much. Love goes the extra mile. Look how handsome your father is."

Rani looked. Sure enough, yes, her father looked very handsome. Particularly from the way he was looking at his wife in that picture.

"Do you see?" she asked Rani.

Rani had nodded. "I see."

"I wish that kind of love for all my girls." Her mother had held her close while Rani bombarded her with questions about her wedding, her job, everything.

A week later, her mother's car was hit by a drunk driver.

Rani never saw that picture again.

Rani wasn't sure why the tears fell, maybe it was all the wedding talk. Her mother had been gone for a long time. But still, she found herself crying over her mother once again, in Param's arms.

Param came over every day after her mother's funeral. He brought their homework and did his and then he did hers. He would talk to Rani about school, but never required her to say a word, for which Rani had been grateful. His presence was balm to her soul, and she found herself looking forward to him coming over every day.

"Today, in English, Mrs. Stuppy passed out our read-

ing assignments." He handed Rani her copy of A Long Walk to Water. *His eyes lit up. "We get to read." A love of books was something they shared, and it wasn't unusual for them to simply sit side by side and read.*

Param sat next to her on the sofa and opened his book, nodding at hers. She had opened her book, intending to read, but the next thing she knew, she was sobbing and Param was holding her tight and murmuring words of comfort.

She had cried herself weak that afternoon, and Param hadn't moved.

The next day, he showed up again and they sat next to each other and read.

Param held Rani while she cried. She hadn't done this in a long while. But one never really got completely over the loss of a loved one.

The rest of the family had gone on to the restaurant.

Shops of all kinds lined both sides of Oak Tree Lane, the main drag in Edison. There were sari stores, stores that sold gold and diamond jewelry that were patrolled by security, shops that sold fake jewelry, stores that were filled with lenghas, Anarkalis, and men's sherwanis. And then there were the restaurants—some that served only street food and chai, to ones that served the fanciest Indian meals. There were grocery stores that sold snacks and kulfi, and everything in between. The streets were full of people huddled up in their winter outerwear, navigating the stores and restaurants and traffic.

The aroma of spices and fried delicacies filled the air.

"Food first," Param said to Rani.

"You always want to eat." Rani wiped away the last of her tears.

"You okay?"

She nodded. "I think seeing all the family together, and all the wedding stuff—real or not—I suppose a girl wants her mother." She shrugged. "I think about her all the time… I wonder what she might think of me, you know?"

"She would be busting with pride," Param said as he enveloped her in a bear hug. He was easily getting used to hugging Rani. She felt so right in his arms. Like that was where she belonged.

"You think?" Rani asked when he pulled back.

"I know."

Her smile was worth more than all the jewelry on this street.

"Come on. Gotta fuel the muscles, girl," he said.

This earned him a chuckle and a light smack on the bicep.

"I could eat." She rolled her eyes at him and they proceeded to meet the rest of the group at the restaurant. Param had a paratha stuffed with potato, onion and spinach. Rani had a similar stuffed flatbread but chose paneer and chili as her filing, and declared it was her favorite. Param tried hers and immediately figured out how to make them.

He'd been cooking as long as he could remember. It probably started because his mother couldn't keep up with his appetite. He hated to constantly be asking her to cook for him—though his brothers seemed to have no problem with this—so he started helping her in the kitchen, letting her teach him her favorite family recipes in the process. It turned into a routine, one that he found soothing and satisfying. Afterall, it was one thing to be able to cook for yourself, but it was something else completely to cook and feed those you loved. Rani would tease him that "touch" was his love language, but the reality was, his love language was food, specifically feeding people.

Feeding Rani.

The table chatter was of nothing else but their upcoming nuptials and what everyone would wear, what food to make and what music to listen to. Karina was taking notes on her phone of what everyone liked and what she should try to make next. Everyone had opinions, and Karina started to pale and appeared overwhelmed by the whole thing. Param leaned over and whispered in her ear.

"Keep it simple. Whatever you make will be amazing."

"I just want it to be special for Rani," Karina said.

"It will be." Param squeezed her hand and she nodded. He looked around the table. "Chai to go. My bride and I need clothes." He glanced at Rani, and she gave a small eye roll only he could see. He suppressed his smile.

As they walked off lunch on their way to the first store, her father and Anil Uncle fell into step with Rani and Param. She shot Param a look. Something was up.

"Beti." Anil Uncle was always calm and composed and this moment was no exception. He ran his gaze over Param and landed on her. Her father stood on her other side. "I spoke with your father about this, and he is in agreement. I know I will be your father-in-law, but your mother was very dear to me. Like a sister."

Rani knew where he was going with this. She threw a panicked look at Param. "Anil Uncle. It's not—"

"Your mother did not have a brother. If she did, he would be buying your wedding clothes for you. We used to joke, the four of us, that when you girls got married, I would play the part of mama. I would have for Karina, and I look forward to doing so one day for Sona. This is my first chance, and it is my pleasure to do that for you, beti."

Rani stood frozen in the street, tears in her eyes—again. She could not allow Param's father to purchase her wedding outfit as if he were her maternal uncle for her *fake marriage*. Param caught her eye and gave her a small smile and a shrug. They had no choice. Keep their eye on the prize.

"I would be honored, Uncle." A tear ran down her cheek. She lost herself in the idea that she really was getting married. This is what her mom would have wanted. "My mom would be thrilled." She glanced at her father, who wiped away a tear as well.

"She would be touched and she would run up a bill for you, my friend," her father chuckled.

"I expect nothing less from her daughter," Anil Uncle said.

"When we are done here today, I insist on a celebratory dinner," her father announced, laughing.

Rani could not remember the last time she heard him give a hearty laugh like that. She caught her sisters' eyes and saw that they had noticed as well. A quick glance at her fiancé told her that he had seen it too.

Chapter Eighteen

They started shopping with a purpose, his mom having them try on various clothes, haggling with store owners over the price. Pankthi noting everything on her spreadsheets. Sona just kept taking pictures of it all.

"Sona, this is just pre-wedding stuff," Rani insisted.

"Yes. But it's good practice for me, and you never know when you might want to remember an outfit or something."

Pre-wedding documentation? Rani shared a look with Param. It was getting out of hand. He gave her the minutest shake of his head. They were in it. Couldn't stop now.

His mom finally found something she liked and sent them each into a dressing room. Rani changed into the long skirt and blouse. Karina helped her with the dupatta since the pleats always got her. But the material in Karina's hands was magical. Her sister tucked and pulled while Rani stood as still as possible.

Lastly, Karina lightly placed the maroon veil atop her head. "Wow. Little sister, you make a beautiful bride." Tears shone in her eyes. "Mom would be so proud. I mean, not just that you're getting married, but of you in general."

Rani let a tear of her own fall. Honestly, was she just going to cry the whole day? "I miss her."

Karina nodded. "A girl shouldn't have to get married without her mom."

They looked at each other in the mirror, neither of them mentioning Karina's elopement. Until Karina finally broke the silence. "I was in a bad place. I was already pregnant. Chirag and I panicked. We thought it was the right thing to do." Karina shrugged. "Maybe if Mom had been around to talk to…" A tear rolled down Karina's cheek. She hastily wiped it away and chuckled. "Look at me, going on about…" She waved a hand. "When you…you, little sister, are gorgeous." She smiled at Rani in the mirror.

Rani turned and gave her big sister a hug, tears streaming down her cheeks. "I do miss Mom. I wish she were here. But I'm really glad you're here. And whatever happened, now we have Veer."

Karina hugged her back. "He is the cutest, isn't he?"

Rani pulled back and grinned. "You make the best babies, Karina Ben."

"Yeah, I do," Karina agreed and Rani saw the happiness in her eyes. "Come on. That groom of yours is out there looking hot all by himself."

Rani stepped off the riser and walked out of the dressing room.

Param was facing the mirror but she knew the exact moment he saw her because he froze, and his eyes went soft.

Param, in his sherwani, made her heart pound in her chest. She could only imagine how much better he would look if it actually fit him. He looked like he was willing his muscles to not rip anything.

Rani wasn't blind. She knew Param was exceedingly handsome. Other women commented about it all the time. To Rani, he was her best friend; she knew his strengths and weaknesses, so she didn't always notice how handsome he was on the outside.

Right now, she noticed.

Funny, she had just seen him dressed as a groom eight months ago, but she didn't remember her heart racing like this, breaking out in a sweat or not wanting to stop looking at him.

If she was being honest, she knew the reason was because this time, right now, she was looking at him dressed as *her* groom, and that made her happy all over.

Though he wasn't really hers, and he never would be. Not like that, anyway. Suddenly, this felt different. Something deeper stirred inside her.

Something that wanted to make Param hers for real.

Param had donned the off-white sherwani that had just a hint of gold threading throughout that his mother handed him. The collar was high, and the buttons were a simple gold. The fit was tight, but that was usually the case.

He'd exited his dressing room before Rani and stood before the giant mirror as instructed. He was fiddling with his buttons and sleeves, so he didn't see Rani until she was next to him.

His heart stopped for a moment, then pounded in his chest. Rani had on a short cream blouse with matching skirt that left her midriff bare and touched the ground. A cream dupatta was loosely wrapped around her and fell from her shoulder to her hip. Gold and red threading and beading accented the outfit. She had a red dupatta on her head as a veil.

Not to say he'd never seen her dressed up, but he had certainly never seen her looking like a bride.

His bride.

And yes, she was *his Rani*. And he could not take his eyes off her.

She stopped and stood next to him, and they looked at each other in the mirror. He met her eyes. They were slightly red-rimmed and swollen from her previous tears, but he suspected she shed a few tears in the dressing room as well. A quick glance at Karina revealed red-rimmed eyes over there as well. He raised an eyebrow at Rani, but she smiled and the glow around her was surreal. She took his breath away.

"Oh. Your turban." His mother came over with a ready-made turban in the same shade of dark red as Rani's veil and handed it to Rani. "Put it on him. Let's see how it looks."

Rani took the turban and looked at him. He bent over, his eyes never leaving hers as she lifted the turban and placed it on his head. Her hands shook, and he took both of her hands in his as he straightened and stepped closer to her. He brought her hands together, covered by his own. Her gaze never left his and he felt her relax into his hands.

"You look—" She gave a small shrug and a smile.

"You too," he said softly. "But even more." He dropped his gaze to her mouth, and her lips parted. He leaned down, ever so slightly toward her. She lifted her chin, ever so subtly toward him, her gaze shifting to his mouth.

He wanted her.

Most definitely not as a friend.

Just then, the turban fell from his head, landing between them. The moment was gone.

"Whoa," he said, laughing and catching the turban.

"Of course you need a bigger size," his mother said. "I'll get it."

Param caught Rani's eye, hoping to still what had passed between them. She held his gaze for a moment, then her eyes hardened, before her sister called to her.

Something had floated between them, something different than friendship. They'd made a deal.

And it had just gotten complicated.

Chapter Nineteen

Try as he might, Param could not erase the image of Rani as a bride from his mind.

As *his* bride.

"How was Edison?" Nishant smirked as he handed Param a bourbon from their father's stash.

"Fine. Great food. Excellent chai." Param sipped the liquid. It warmed him.

"I meant wedding shopping." Nishant took a healthy sip of his bourbon and led the way to their family room. He sat on the sofa.

Param shrugged and followed, sitting in a chair next to Nishant. "Fine."

"You don't seem excited."

"I'm excited. Of course I am. Who wouldn't be excited about marrying Rani? She's amazing." He grinned. She really was.

"I mean, I wouldn't be excited if I were fake marrying my best friend to get money for my little brother's experimental treatment," Nishant said casually.

Param froze. "What? Why would you say that—Rani and I are—I mean, that's not fair." Param took another tact and laughed. "You're good. Almost had me going."

Nishant stared at him. "So, you're really in love with Rani?"

"Duh. Of course. Why wouldn't I be? She's beautiful and smart and funny, and she doesn't let me get away with anything. She's everything good in my life." All true. "And if there's ever anything bad, she helps make it better. I wouldn't know who I was without her."

"She's your best friend." Nishant still sounded skeptical.

"Which makes it even better, right?"

"Yeah… I suppose. It just seemed a bit too convenient. You two being together right when Milan needed you to be." Nishant focused on Param.

Param leaned toward Nishant, taking another sip of his drink. "You want the truth?"

"The truth would be fabulous." Nishant leaned in.

Here it was, he was finally going to have to give the "how it happened" story. Param looked his older brother in the eye. Start with the truth, then…embellish. "The truth is that Rani and I—it's been going on for a bit. Remember she came to the islands with me?"

"Yes. After the whole Sangeeta fiasco." He waved a dismissive hand.

"Right." Param paused. "We had a great time together—so much better than going alone or not going at all." It was true, he would have been lost if he had gone alone, and he would have gone out of his mind if he had stayed. "That last night, we had a lot to drink…

I kissed her. And she kissed me back." He'd never had a kiss like that. And he'd almost been married.

"You what?" Nishant's eyes widened.

"We kissed. And it was amazing. I had no idea that we felt that way about each other until we kissed." It was true—at least for him. He'd experienced feelings for Rani that he had never experienced before. Maybe the alcohol had helped instigate that kiss, but the feelings—his feelings—had been real in that moment. The kiss had felt natural, right. He remembered wanting more—so much more—but being afraid what would happen if they explored those emotions, if they allowed their friendship to change like that.

There were times when he feared that he would never have what his brothers had found. He had thought Sangeeta was the one. He had even taken a break from her for a couple weeks to be sure. During those two weeks, he had come to the conclusion Sangeeta must be the one.

And then Sangeeta ran.

And he wasn't sure about anything.

Until he kissed Rani. That was it, wasn't it? Kissing Rani felt right, like nothing else in his life had. She was his best friend, but kissing her had opened up a deeper connection between them than he'd ever thought possible.

When Rani had shut him down when he tried to talk to her about it, he accepted that because he didn't want to lose what they already had for the possibility of what might be. One woman had already left him. He couldn't stand to lose Rani as well.

But the truth was, there were times when he ached to hold her like that again, to kiss her like that again, to lose himself to her. Like when she put on bridal clothes. Or held his hand. Or melted into him. Or simply existed.

Oh.

No.

"Then what?" Nishant sipped his drink.

Param shrugged. Now for the extra. "We've been together since. We didn't say anything because I had literally just been left at the mandap. We were giving it time, to see where it was going, before we involved the families, you know?"

Nishant nodded. That, he understood.

"Then when we realized it could help Milan, we told you all." It was easier than he'd thought.

"Okay. Just checking." Nishant finished his drink. "Why?"

"Because we need this money for Milan. And we can't afford to mess this up because you and Rani have some scheme going. Patel Dada will see right through you. He's being extra diligent because of the whole Sangeeta thing."

"Scheme?" Param feigned ignorance.

"Don't give me that look. You two schemed plenty. Remember when you tried to get a puppy?"

Param bit his cheeks to keep from laughing. They had taken a puppy from a neighbor whose dog had given birth and presented it to their parents as if it were a lost stray. Needless to say, they were found out and were forced to return the puppy.

Param forced a huge smile. "You do not have to worry. No scheme. Marriage isn't exactly a puppy, you jackass. This is the real deal. Only true love." A warm sappy feeling came over him when he said the words "true love."

Odd.

Nishant nodded. "It's about time. You two are meant to be together. I'm just happy you both finally see it." He glanced at his watch. "Sorry, I need to go. Pankthi had a great time today. She's completely in her element: Boss Lady."

Param nodded, the smile fixed to his face. He did not trust his voice at the moment. He waited for Nishant to leave and collapsed on the sofa. Meant to be together? They were friends. Best friends. No matter what feelings he might have temporarily had or not had, in Rani's case.

His phone dinged. A text from Rani. Meet me in the cul-de-sac.

Chapter Twenty

Rani was lying on the sofa after a very successful but full day in Edison. Sona was seated next to her and they were watching *Friends* reruns. Karina joined in, plopping in between them after putting Veer to bed. She had a chilled bottle of wine and three glasses.

"Well, that was a day." Karina poured them each a glass and held hers up for a toast. "To my littlest sister. Congratulations! We're so happy for you."

They clinked glasses and drank deeply.

"Even if you didn't tell us you were dating your best friend," Karina added with a small scowl.

"We were waiting for the right time. We wanted to see where it all was going before we involved the families," Rani said.

"Whatever." Sona waved Karina off and squeezed Rani's hand. "We all saw this coming—I'm just happy it finally happened."

They all kept saying that. That she and Param were always going to get together. She'd never thought that. Not ever.

Well, maybe not never.

She may have thought it when she'd had that crush on him senior year of high school. She might have had that thought after that kiss on their last night in the islands. Something had stirred inside her, but by morning she had squashed it right back down where it belonged—in a tiny little box in the back of her head. Param was her best friend, her rock. He was there when no one else was, even her sisters. He had helped her through that awful time when her mother died, not to mention always being there for her, through med school, residency, all of it. No way was she going to risk losing that bond because something had "stirred" during a it-should-never-have-happened kiss. Not to mention, after watching her father lose his soulmate, Rani was determined to keep that little bit of distance between her and Param.

"I wish I had what you have," Sona continued.

"Wait, what?" Karina said, sharing a look with Rani. Rani sat up straight and they both turned toward their sister.

"I'm not an idiot." Sona shrugged.

"What…does that mean?" Karina treaded carefully, while Rani kept her mouth shut for the moment.

Sona rolled her eyes. "You know. You both know."

"You mean how you and Steve have no chemistry and really shouldn't be together no matter how great he is in bed?" Rani couldn't help from blurting it out. A pit grew in her stomach as she watched tears form in Sona's eyes. Oh, crap. She should have kept her mouth shut. Karina nudged her shoulder accusingly.

"I mean… I didn't mean that." Rani tried to take it back. "I have no idea how he is in bed."

"Rani!" Karina scolded.

"No, it's okay," a teary Sona said. "She's right. That's why I'm crying."

"Oh, sweetie." Karina put her glass down and wrapped her arms around Sona. That was Karina. She was a natural mother. Probably because she filled that role for them when their mother died.

Rani put down her glass and joined the sister hug. Karina and Sona each wrapped an arm around her. Sona pulled back after a moment and Karina produced tissues from basically nowhere and Sona wiped her eyes.

"Sona, you need to break up with him. He's a great guy. Maybe just not for you," Rani said.

"Everyone doesn't get a relationship like you and Param." She eyed Karina. "Or even Mom and Papa."

"It's true," agreed Karina.

Rani had to hold herself back from saying, "You mean fake?" The three of them were a mess.

"But no one was like Mom and Papa," Karina said. She was right. Their parents had set a pretty high standard.

"Hey, don't you think that maybe we remember them differently than they really were?" Rani asked.

"I don't know," Karina said. "It's been over fifteen years and Papa has never even dated. He says she was his only love."

"Yeah. But Papa is not old. He might want to share his life with someone," Rani said

"He has us," Karina stated as fact as only a firstborn child could.

"It's not the same," added Sona.

"So, what is the deal with you and Steve?" Karina asked.

Sona shrugged. "I don't know. It was fun, reconnecting, but sometimes I feel like all we have is our connection from the past, from high school. What about now? I'm not the person I was in high school."

"Thank god," Karina and Rani chorused.

Sona just rolled her eyes. "I mean, who are we moving forward?"

Karina and Rani stared at their sister. She was not the philosophical one. So, this was serious. "Sona, he doesn't have to be the one," Karina said. "I jumped into my marriage too fast. Take your time. Papa wants you to be happy."

"But how will I know if he is the one?" Sona asked.

"Don't ask me." Karina shook her head. "Ask the sister who knows."

Both sisters turned to Rani. "What? You want me to tell you how I know he's the one?"

"Well, yes. You two are clearly made to be together," Karina said. She sounded a little bit jealous.

Rani stared at them. They were legit waiting for her to say something, to impart wisdom. "Well, he brings me dinner when I work at the clinic. And many times at the ED. He always cleans up after, too, so I can get back to patients or even take a ten-minute power nap."

"Super sweet but he has always done that," Sona said.

That was true. Rani grinned. He'd been doing that the whole time she was a resident. Four years. It was possible that he and Sangeeta had had an argument about it once. Rani couldn't be sure.

Rani sat back and sipped her wine. "He answers my texts as soon as he sees them, even if it's just with an emoji or something. He never forgets my birthday, always a card or flowers or…" She grinned.

"What?"

"A book." She nearly giggled. "And I have missed his once or twice."

"All adorable, but how did you know you could spend your life with him?" Sona pressed.

Rani stared at her sisters. She didn't know that. But she did know she could never envision her life without him. "I just know that I can't imagine my life without him in it. He *gets* me. And I get him. He's my rock." It was the truth. Next to her sisters and Papa, Param was the most important person in her life. "He means the world to me."

"Yeah, but what kind of kisser is he?" Sona asked, then downed her wine and poured more all around, lightening the mood. "Seriously."

He was an amazing kisser. She only knew from that one time, but she had lost herself in him for those moments, wine or no wine. Rani flushed.

"Oh my god. Our baby sister is blushing. I didn't think I'd live to see the day." Karina laughed.

Rani could not remember the last time she'd heard Karina laugh. She was so busy with Veer and work that there was rarely any downtime like this, where they could just laugh. And be sisters.

"He is a damn good kisser, if you must know," Rani said, still flushing. If one kiss can tell that.

"And…?" Sona smirked.

"And what?" asked Rani.

"And how is he in bed? What else?" Sona pushed, and Karina rolled her eyes, but she turned her attention on Rani all the same.

Rani lost her breath for a moment. She had no idea and quite frankly had never considered what kind of lover her best friend, Param Sheth, might be. There were certain things you simply did not ask yourself. But here were her sisters asking her how her fiancé was in bed. If they were really engaged, she'd have an answer for this. She had no answer. But now she had all sorts of images in her head that she'd never had before. Naked images. And they weren't necessarily unpleasant.

"Um…well…" she started, clearing her throat. "You've seen him, all tall and muscular, not to mention he's the sweetest guy ever. So how do you think he is in bed?" Rani held her breath, hoping the ploy would work.

"I knew it," Sona nearly gasped. "It's mind-blowing, right?"

Rani simply grinned, but her heart rate increased significantly. Mind-blowing? Oh, boy.

"Honestly, I'm jealous," Karina said. "I can't remember the last time I had sex. Not that it matters, I'm too damn tired to do anything but fall asleep after I put Veer to bed."

Rani laughed with her sisters. "Seriously, Sona. If it doesn't feel right now, it won't feel right later." Not that she should be giving out advice.

"I know. But you know how Papa is."

They did. After their mother died he did his best to be both parents, even when it was uncomfortable for all of them. Like when he took them to buy birth control and talked to them about being respected and making good choices. He met all their boyfriends, but never did the "dad thing" in giving them a hard time. Instead he tried to get to know them, so he would know what kind of person his daughters were hanging out with.

When Karina came home pregnant and married to Chirag, Papa did have a bit of a fit. But he had been more upset that Karina hadn't come to him as opposed to the fact that she was pregnant and now married. After that, Papa had supported her, and when Chirag left to "find himself," not one "I told you so" left his mouth.

But the thing was that since their mother died, he seemed to have two goals for them each. Education and marriage. Their mother had always wanted them to get married, and so it seemed their father was making sure her dream came true.

"Sona." Rani reached out and took her sister's hand. "Papa will be fine. You should not marry someone just because he wants you 'settled.'"

Sona pulled her hand away. "I'm the fuck-up in the family. I haven't finished college and I'm over thirty. I've been through any number of boyfriends. Getting married is the only right thing I can do at this point."

"Sona, you are one of the smartest people I know. You're amazing with art and fashion, and you'll be done with college in literally one more class. You don't need to get married for Papa. Especially if he's not the right guy," Rani said.

"Easy for you to say. You're the baby," Sona countered.

Rani saw Karina nodding her head in agreement with Sona's statement. Well, they didn't have to worry about her being the favorite for much longer. As soon as Rani married Param and they got the money, they would divorce within a month. Let's see what Papa thought about that.

Chapter Twenty-One

Rani's conversation with her sisters was bugging her out. She needed to talk to Param. In person. She put on her coat and boots and went to meet him in the area they called the cul-de-sac. This was really just a small area of a walking path that was unlit. They used to bring flashlights and meet here as children to play hide-and-seek with the neighborhood children. She was a grown woman, a doctor, getting married, meeting her fiancé (fake though he may be), and she was somehow nervous.

"Hey," he called from the dark as she approached.

"Hey," she said, shivering. The conversation with her sisters really must have been getting under skin, because her first thought was how handsome he looked in the moonlight.

Param unwrapped his scarf from his neck and wrapped it around her. He'd been doing that for years. She accepted the added warmth. "What's up?"

"What are we doing?" Rani asked.

"We are helping Milan," Param stated firmly.

She shook her head. "We are lying to our families. They think we are together for real."

"As they should," Param answered. "Since that is what we have told them."

"No. They always thought we should be together and now they think we are. It's like we are fulfilling their dreams," Rani continued.

"Rani, Milan had a seizure in the car on the way home from the hospital. He has a small seizure every couple days. Aisha is afraid to leave him home alone." Param sighed.

Rani knew this. They were all on the same text chain together.

"It's going to keep happening," Param continued. "This fake marriage was your idea, but the more we get into this, the more I think we can sell it." He paused and moved closer to her. He smelled of sage, which was the cologne she had given him, and she welcomed the heat from his body, leaning into it, an oasis in the frigid cold. "But if you're not up for this, we can stop it. Right now. We go home and tell everyone we're not getting married, and we'll get the money from somewhere else." He rested a cool finger on her chin and bent a little so he could see her eyes. He was so damn tall. "It's okay. Our friendship will never change."

Rani took in Param, her gentle giant. "No. I'm good. Just having a minor freak-out. I just need to keep my eye on the prize."

"You sure? It's not like you to have a crisis of conscience."

"It's not like you to not have one." She chuckled. "Remember the puppy?"

She heard him groan in the dark. It was actually more of a low growl. "Let it go already. We were ten. And yes, I remember. I freaked out because we were lying to the family about the fact that he was a stray. Mrs. Wilson lived three doors down. Everyone knew her dog had puppies. It wouldn't have taken much to get caught."

"Says you." She chided him. "You told before we even had a chance. If you'd let it ride, one of us might have had a dog." She barely kept the bitterness from her voice. It had been a great plan and Param had messed it up.

"What's the point?" Param asked softly.

"The point is I don't want to mess this up," Rani said.

"You won't. I won't let you. We're in this together. You said it yourself. We know each other better than anyone. It shouldn't be hard for us to convince everyone that we're in love."

"Rani!" Sona was calling out to her from the back porch. "Karina, why isn't the light working?"

Before she knew what was happening, Param had pulled her into his body, and smashed his mouth onto hers, kissing her. Without conscious thought, she opened her mouth to him and kissed him back, pressing her body against his. He moved his hand to rest against her cheek, which seemed to bring some control back to him, and his kisses became gentle and soft as opposed to desperate and needy. Though Rani couldn't find fault with any of them. Rani pushed her lips against his, her tongue searching for his. Forget gentle, this was amazing. Param tilted her head back and deepened their kiss as if all he'd ever wanted was to kiss her senseless in this backyard, in the middle of winter.

How long they kissed like that, Rani had no idea. She was living in that moment and hoping it never ended. Breathing was really not a priority.

The backyard light went on. Param made no move to stop kissing her, so she went with it.

"It's just Param and Rani making out in the backyard," Sona called.

Reluctantly, she stopped kissing him, but they remained entwined in each other's arms, squinting in the light.

"Sorry. Resume." Sona went back inside, switching off the light.

"Rani?" he whispered in the dark, his mouth near her ear, his soft voice sending shivers down her body.

She leaned her cheek into his face, the scruff on his face was right now her favorite texture in the world. "Mmm?" she said because speech was currently not among the things she could control right now.

He cleared his throat and lifted his head away from hers. She held back the reflexive whimper that built inside her. She cleared her throat as well and looked up at him. Lips swollen, eyes glazed, he looked as dazed as she felt.

"Um. Well." She cleared her throat. "Very convincing. They would have wondered why we were conversing outside. In the dark." Every part of her wanted to lose herself in that kiss again.

Param nodded. "Right." They were whispering as if talking in normal tones would erase the moment. He met her eyes and looked at her like he was more than ready to lose himself in that kiss again as well.

"I should go," she said. "Back in."

Param nodded again. Apparently speaking was a challenge. Seemed only fair, her knees were weak and her legs wouldn't move.

"Good night, Rani," he said softly.

Wow. He could speak, but the way he said her name... she needed to go. She forced her legs to move away from him. "I'll talk to you later."

Chapter Twenty-Two

His mom was throwing an engagement party. In her house. It wasn't enough that he was getting married in a few weeks, she was having a party anyway. And she hadn't bothered to inform him until the day before.

"Mom," he said as she handed him clothes to wear for the party. "An engagement party is not necessary. The wedding is literally in three weeks." Rani was not going to be happy about this. "What did Rani say about this?"

"She was excited, very touched that we are doing this for you both. It will be fun. I just slapped it altogether anyway." She beamed at him. She was wearing a beautiful pink sari with a simple gold border. "This is a simple kurta set. You'll be comfortable, I promise."

"Did you get—"

"I have your measurements," she said before he could

finish. "The length is correct." She chuckled. "Get dressed and come down."

Param did as he was told, and by the time he came down, half the town was at his house. Except for his bride.

"Where is she?" he asked his mother as he grabbed a dabeli.

"She'll be here soon enough." His mother shook her head at him. "Patience." She shared a look with her sister who was assembling the dabeli sandwiches. "See, Ritu Ben? Young love cannot wait." They both chuckled. "And see? The way he calls her 'she' because there could only be one 'she' that he was talking about." Param flushed and took another dabeli before leaving the kitchen.

Milan and Aisha were looking very nice in their coordinating outfits—she in a navy sari and he in a matching kurta. He couldn't help but to keep watching Milan, making sure he was okay. His attention was moved only when they heard a commotion at the door. He and Milan shrugged at each other but went to the door behind Aisha to see what was up.

Nishant and Pankthi had arrived, and right behind them were Rani's sisters and father. Pulling up the rear was Rani.

If Rani had looked amazing in Edison just donning her panetar, she was resplendent right now. She was in a sage green lengha that highlighted the brown of her skin and the deep brown of her eyes. The lengha looked as though it was cut to fit her body, accentuating her curves in the most beautiful way. Her hair flowed in soft curls around her.

He had always appreciated that Rani was an attractive woman, so it was no surprise to him that in this moment she radiated beauty. What did surprise him was the way his heart pounded in his chest, the way his palms sweated, and how he felt frozen to his spot in that moment. How he was taken by the beauty of this woman, whose face and expressions lived inside him. He had no idea what his face showed, but he never wanted to leave that moment.

"Rani," he said softly. And the whole crowd turned to look at him. He was vaguely aware of giggles and sighs from their family and friends, but his focus was on *her*.

"Param," she said, smiling right at him.

What was the matter with him? This was Rani. His best friend. And they were putting on a show. Or at least that's what they were supposed to be doing. But whatever was going on inside him right now was not a show.

"You look…" He raised his eyebrows and shook his head.

"The English teacher has no words," Rani chided, and the crowd laughed.

"I have no words," he confessed.

She came to him and took his hand. He leaned down and kissed her as if it were the most natural thing in world. Because kissing her in that moment was the most natural thing in the world. Forget the fact that he had thought of nothing else since his mom told him about the engagement party. Ever since that kiss in the backyard, he was like a teenager, and he suddenly seemed to be focused on opportunities to kiss Rani. And have her kiss him back like this.

Because she kissed him back with her whole self. She couldn't possibly be completely faking, not with a kiss like that.

A small voice tried to remind him that this was fake, but he squashed that voice. She had wanted to kiss him. He could feel it. He certainly had wanted to kiss her.

He was still lying awake at night thinking about it. Thinking about her. He still wasn't sure if he was ready—or willing?—to date other people, but he certainly had no problem envisioning Rani as *his*.

"Come on in," Nishant called out. "It's cold by the door. Mom and Dad have food, and I'll be tending bar."

This was met with a chorus of agreement as people moved away from the entrance way and into the house. Param gently pressed his hand on the small of her back to keep her where they were.

When they were alone, he looked at her.

"You—"

"Nicely done," Rani interrupted. "You looked completely smitten. It was perfect. I hope I was as convincing as you. Especially since Patel Dada is here. And nice touch with that kiss."

Nice touch? Wait. Param snapped his head around. How had he missed Patel Dada? "What?"

"Patel Dada came in with Nishant. Didn't you see him? Anyway. You played your part perfectly." She grinned and stepped back to look at him. "And you clean up quite nicely, Param Sheth."

"You look incredible," he said softly.

She took his hand. "Save it for Patel Dada." She tugged his hand. "Come on."

He followed her into the house. Music was playing from the speakers, Nishant was ensuring that everyone had a drink, and Milan was passing around appetizers. The party was in full swing.

Nishant stopped over and handed them each a bourbon on ice. The liquid was smooth and cool as it went down, relaxing all his muscles. He was hyper-aware of Rani beside him like he'd never been before. They greeted their friends, accepting congratulations easily. Rani was glowing, she seemed to be genuinely enjoying herself, and she never left his side.

"So how did you finally get together?" Patel Dada asked over the crowd, and the room went silent as everyone focused on them.

Rani looked at him, and wrapped her arm around his waist. "Oh. One day, we realized that we had feelings that were deeper than friendship."

"There's usually a moment," one of the aunties piped up.

"Go on, Param. Tell them about the kiss." Nishant raised his bourbon to them.

Murmuring floated across the room at this news.

"The first one in the Caribbean," Nishant prodded him on.

Param was going to prod him. "Yes. That kiss…was amazing," Param finally said, but at the same time that Rani spoke.

"Oh, that kiss wasn't anything," Rani said, giggling.

He looked at her. They just contradicted one another. With Patel Dada in the room.

Rani shook her head. "What my fiancé means," she intertwined her fingers with his, "is that the kiss in the Caribbean was the moment for him. But it took me a bit more time to come around." She grinned around the room. "I had to make sure I wasn't the rebound girl, right?" This was met with laughter.

"There is no way you're the rebound girl," Param spoke without thinking. "I knew it then." He looked at her. "And I know it now," he said softly. The truth of the words struck him.

"Well, that is good to know." She chuckled and pulled him close. He let himself be pulled into her, draping an arm around her and enjoying the feel of her against him.

"Come on now," one of the aunties said jovially. "Every couple has a story."

Except they did not. A general chorus of "Yes, yes, let's hear it," and the crowd went silent in anticipation. Param glanced at Rani and saw panic in her eyes.

He cleared his throat. "Well, as I told my brother, we shared a kiss in the islands, but at the time, both of us agreed that it was a mistake that never should have happened. We didn't want to ruin years of friendship over a misbegotten kiss." He shrugged. "We chalked it up to alcohol and broken hearts." He nodded at Rani, and she nodded back, a smile on her face. He knew almost all the faces she made and almost all of her smiles. This was one of the fake smiles, but her eyes approved of his story.

"Well, at least she did." He paused. *Start with the truth, then expand...* "I, however, could not stop thinking about that moment. But she was my best friend and I had just come out of a broken engagement, so the timing did not seem ideal. So, I let it go." He looked at her, still in his arms as if that were the most natural place for her to be. She smiled and nodded encouragement.

"At least I tried to." He paused, still looking at her. "But you know how love can be. It sneaks up on you sometimes when you least expect it." He moved aside a small lock of her hair that had fallen near her eye, grazing his finger over the skin of her cheek. Her soft gasp at his touch was real, and his mouth went dry.

He swallowed. "The more time I spent with Rani, the more time I wanted to spend with her." Rani was flushed, her eyes never leaving his. It was as if he were telling only her this story.

"I wasn't sure I was in love with her until she kissed me again one night. Then I knew. I knew she was the one for me." He forgot in that moment that at least hundred people watched them. There was only the two of them, and he had just revealed feelings he hadn't even been sure he had.

There was a beat of silence, until someone whistled, and the guests clapped and cheered them on. Brought back suddenly to reality, Param gathered himself and winked at Rani, while she melted into him. "That was perfect," she whispered. "Very believable. Who knew you had it in you?" she said so only he could hear.

"I am an English teacher," he quipped, kissing the top of her head. "I know a little something about storytelling."

She looked up at him, impressed. "That you do," she said before turning to their guests who were coming over to hug them. She held on to his hand.

Every good lie stems from truth. The words echoed in his head as he watched her greet their friends. He shook the thought from his mind. There was no truth in the story he told.

Was there?

Patel Dada approached them making eye contact with Param. "Well, it is good to see that you appear happy."

His choice of words did not get past Param. "We are happy, Patel Dada." He squeezed her hand and brought it to his lips. His heart thumped when a small sigh escaped her as he kissed her hand. The party wore on, people sang songs, danced and celebrated.

Param found himself alone with Rani on the dance floor, which was really his mom's living room. She fit easily into his arms and they danced in sync with one another.

"Nicely done," Rani said so softly that only he could hear.

"You too," he said quietly, focusing in on her so completely that he was no longer aware of the guests around them. "I hope Patel Dada believed us."

"I'm sure he did," Rani assured him.

"I don't know, he gave me a look."

"You're being paranoid. We are a hit. Now, how did Nishant know about that kiss?" she asked, moving closer to him. "I'd forgotten about that."

Forgotten? The pang of disappointment that shot through him at that word was physically painful. Of course she didn't remember, she didn't want to. But no way had she actually forgotten. He knew her better than that.

Or did he?

Param managed to gather himself enough to speak. "He asked how we got together." He shrugged.

"So you told him we kissed? You couldn't come up with something better?" she chided him.

"It was the first thing I thought of," Param replied. Because he thought about that kiss all the time. "Besides, all lies have a basis in truth, right?"

"Makes sense. That kiss was pretty...real." She glanced at him then behind him.

He chuckled softly. "I knew you hadn't forgotten."

She shrugged one arm. "What difference does it make? The kiss served its real purpose here tonight. It gave us a story."

Param stared at her. She had just dismissed that kiss as if it were nothing to her. He managed to keep his expression neutral. "Right. A story."

Chapter Twenty-Three

Rani needed to get out of this lengha. It was starting to itch, and her feet hurt in the heels she had borrowed from Sona. But Param's story had everyone a little teary-eyed with happiness and everyone needed to hug them. She was caught up in the excitement of it all and lost track of time.

Param came to her side and rested his hand on her elbow as he leaned down to whisper in her ear. "I thought you needed to be at the clinic."

Goosebumps went down that side of her body from his voice and breath, so it took Rani a moment to register his words.

"Oh! I do. What time is it?"

"Three."

She turned to face him. "I need to be there by four. I was hoping we'd be done by three."

"It's fine. You're a doctor. You can go."

"It's not weird for a bride to leave her engagement party?" Rani asked.

"Not if you're a doctor."

"Right." Rani was so caught up in their "story," it took her a moment to remember the truth. Though if she was honest, the line between story and reality was more blurred than ever. A part of her wanted to stay and revel in the excitement of the day, continue being Param's fiancée. But work called. "I should go."

Param nodded. "I'll take you to your house to change. Everyone will think we simply cannot be apart."

"Sure." Rani shrugged as if she were indifferent to whether he came with her or not, but she wasn't ready to leave his side. A few moments with just Param and no audience might be nice.

Param drove her to her house and waited while she changed into scrubs, wiped off her makeup and tied her hair in a ponytail. She came downstairs. "Thank you. But I should just drive myself so I can go home whenever."

Param was staring at her.

"Param?"

He started. "Sorry. You know, we've known each other so long that I sometimes forget how beautiful you are."

She flushed. "There's no one here to hear you, Param. Storytime is over. Besides, I just took off all the makeup."

"You look…" his smile and words were genuine, "just gorgeous, either way."

Pleasure coursed through her, though she hardly

wanted to acknowledge that Param's words made her feel that way. She raised an eyebrow at him. "You okay? Maybe you had too much drink. I'm not sure that you should be driving."

Param laughed, his natural, true laugh that Rani loved. "No. I'm sober. I just had that one Nishant gave me at the beginning. You know me better than that."

Rani nodded. She did. Her mom had died in a DUI, so drinking and driving was a trigger for her. It was a trigger for both families, actually. She had been driving home from her clinic across town, late one night, when she was hit head on by someone driving in the wrong lane.

"Maybe I'm just getting caught up in the hype of it all." He paused. "But it doesn't change the fact that you are truly beautiful to me."

He didn't say she was truly beautiful, he said she was truly beautiful *to him*. Which seemed to make all the difference to her heart as it thudded in her chest. His words made her feel unexpectedly light, and a large smile and flush fell over her face even as she tried to roll her eyes at him. "Whatever."

"I'll see you later, fiancée," Param called as he left her house.

"You got it, love," Rani called back. She could have sworn Param froze in the doorway for a quick second before leaving. But she could not be sure.

Rani arrived at the clinic still floating from Param's words. She reprimanded herself for acting like a teenager, but even so, she couldn't stop smiling. She parked, made sure to lock her car, and hunched over in the cold wind as she ran into the clinic.

"Hey, Doc," called out Cami as she entered the building. "We have heat today."

Rani nodded. "Let's get Lisa and triage. I'll get some hot cocoa going."

Rani saw the patients that Lisa said were actually sick, and they gave hot cocoa to the ones who just needed a place to be warm. Rani had given out blankets in years past, but there was no budget for that now. She checked her email for a response from the hospital grant committee. Nothing yet.

Four hours later, the waiting room had emptied, and it was time to lock up. Rani sat in the back working on charts.

Cami came in. "Your fiancé is here."

Rani looked up to see Param walking through the door. He was a sight for sore eyes.

She was struck for a moment how truly handsome he was, more so today, even in his winter coat, hoodie, and worn-in blue jeans. The floaty feeling returned and she was happy to see him.

"Hey. I have my car," Rani said.

"I know. Just needed to get out of the house." He took off his coat and sat down across from her. He brought with him some of the bitter cold from outside which contrasted with how warm and wonderful he smelled. Still the sage from his cologne, but also smoke, as if they'd done a bonfire.

"Bonfire at the party?" Rani looked at the time on her phone.

"No. Yes. It's the after-party."

"Cami, go on. I'll lock up." Rani called out.

"You got it, Doc." She heard the door shut behind Cami.

"I brought sandwiches," he said as he pulled a brown bag from his backpack.

"Which is the real reason I'm going to marry you," Rani said, snatching the bag.

Param just sat and talked while she ate. He caught her up on all the gossip from the engagement party, who was with whom, what they were saying about them.

Rani just ate and enjoyed his company. This was them. Relaxed, open sharing. All that kissing, that was to help Milan. Though, the kissing was nice. At the party, he'd tasted like bourbon. Which was different from the kiss in the cul-de-sac, where he had tasted more like…chai masala. Which had been different from the kiss in the islands, which had been salty from the oysters and tangy from the wine. The one thing they all had in common was that she hadn't wanted any of them to end.

Param was laughing as he told her the latest in an ongoing saga about one of his cousins. She laughed with him. *This* was the real them. Simple. And easy.

No need to complicate things with kisses.

When Rani's mother died, her father closed down, not crying or showing any kind of emotion. He went to work, claiming he had patients that needed to be seen.

Being the youngest, Rani was very close to her father, so while losing her mother was devastating, her father's distance wrecked her. Param went over every night and did her homework for a few days, until one day he made Rani do her own homework, whether she felt like it or not. "How will you get into college?"

Three months of Param helping her get her homework done, three months of their family and friends bringing them food that her father never touched, and one night Param showed up with his parents.

Anil Uncle was one of her father's closest friends, but he hadn't returned any of Uncle's calls or texts. In fact, her father did not interact with anyone that Rani knew of.

They sent Param and Rani to her room, where her sisters joined them,, and they talked to her father. Rani and her sisters listened with Param from the top of the stairs as Anil Uncle and Veena Auntie laid out what was happening to his family. Karina was feeding everyone, making sure that Rani and Sona got to school and was basically running the house when she should have gone back to college.

"So what?" Karina had whispered, and glared at Param.

Sona was not actually attending any classes and was on her third boyfriend in three months. Sona had actually growled at Param. "Mind your own business."

Rani had nightmares—she, too, glared at Param for telling her secret.

Rani turned on Param and screamed at him. "I can't believe you told your parents. We are fine. My dad loves us. He just misses my mom. You don't know, because no one in your family died." She was seething at him, tears streaming down her face when her father called her name for the first time in three months. She turned

*around to find him standing at the bottom of the steps,
Param's parents behind him.*

"Papa."

"Rani." *He looked like he was crying.* "Karina. Sona."

"Are you crying, Papa?" *Rani had asked.*

"I am. I miss your mother so very much." *Tears were
falling in rivulets down her father's face.*

"Me too, Papa. Me too."

"Do you think we could just miss her together?"
he asked.

*She nodded, realizing that they were completely alone.
Just the four of them. Param and his family had left.*

*Things were different after that night. She, her father,
and her sisters went into therapy, and while it wasn't
always easy, they made progress as a family. Karina
still ran things, Sona still went through boyfriends, and
Rani still avoided commitment.*

*But while they laughed and lived, the overall sad-
ness in her father never really left. He simply filled his
days with everyone else's happiness, so as to ignore
his own loneliness. Rani watched him suffer from the
pain of losing her mother, and she determined that she
would never suffer that fate. It did not seem as though it
was better to have loved and lost. It seemed like it was
better to never really love. To never give your heart to
anyone completely.*

*The day after she had screamed at Param, he showed
up at her front door in the morning to walk to the bus
stop, same as always.*

"I'm sorry I was mean," *Rani had started to apologize. Param stopped her.*

"You're right. I haven't lost anyone like you have.

But you're my best friend, and I'll always just be here, looking out for you."

"Right back at you," Rani had said.

"I know," Param answered.

Chapter Twenty-Four

"Settle down, hyenas. You too, Mufasa. Nala, seriously? I just said to settle down. I need little Simba, front and center, along with Pumba and Timon. We're doing 'Hakuna Matata' right now. Teen Simba and Teen Nala prepare for 'Can You Feel the Love Tonight.' Ms. Vasquez will help you with the song." Param was back in his element.

The children organized themselves as he and Ms. Vasquez went over the choreography of the love scene.

"I don't think we want twelve-year-olds rolling around all over each other, even if they are supposed to be lions," Angelina was saying.

"I agree. Maybe just the circling then?" Param suggested.

"Sounds better." Angelina chuckled. "I can only imagine the emails from the parents."

There was a huge commotion on the stage just then.

The children were catcalling and "oooo-ing." Param was confused.

"Mr. Sheth," Trina sing-songed. "Your best friend is here."

Param turned and sure enough, Rani was making her way toward him, down the aisle. The irony was not lost on him. The sight of her put a smile on his face, as it always did. Today there was just a little something extra. His heart actually pounded in his chest at the sight of her. He might even be sweating a bit.

Something different must have shown on his face, because Angelina raised a perfectly manicured eyebrow at him. "I thought you said she was just your best friend."

Param was still a bit lost watching Rani say hello to all the children who had bombarded her. "She's my fiancée, actually," he said before he realized what he was saying.

"You're engaged?" She narrowed those big brown eyes at him.

Oh, crap. He turned to Angelina. Her mouth was set and there was some anger in her eyes. Deserved because hadn't he been flirting with her a bit in an effort to not be the "groom who was stood up", and he asked her out. "Um…yes. It's a long story." Param kept shifting his eyes to Rani, which really didn't help.

"I'll bet it is." Angelina's voice went cold.

Rani finally reached them and gave him a quick kiss on the lips. The contact was electrifying and calming all at the same time. It also wasn't totally necessary since there was no family around, so Param had the distinct feeling that Rani's kiss was for Angelina's benefit.

Huh.

"Hi, Ms. Vasquez." Rani smiled. "How are the children today?"

Angelina shifted her gaze from Rani to Param. "They're just fine." Her tone continued to be decidedly cooler than prior to Rani's arrival. "I'll just go get the kids started on this part." She eyed Param and walked away.

"Wow. What was that?" Rani asked.

"That was the result of me finally asking a woman out, and then getting 'engaged' to you." He used his fingers as air quotes.

Rani's jaw dropped a bit, but he caught her grin behind it. "Oops."

He pressed his lips together and shook his head. "'Oops' is right."

"Well, I only have thirty minutes before I get on shift. How can I help?" Rani asked.

"Did you just kiss your best friend, Mr. Sheth?" Trevor seemed horrified at the prospect.

"Yes, Trevor, I did. Because we're getting married." It felt completely natural to Param to say that.

"You're marrying your best friend?" This was said with supreme disgust.

"That's the best way," Amy said. "Then you know you like each other. Right, Mr. Sheth?"

Malini came up to them. She eyed Rani. "You don't have a ring."

"I'll be getting her one soon, Malini," Param explained.

Malini pressed her lips together and walked away.

"You leave a trail of broken hearts," Rani said as she watched the young girl walk away.

Param felt himself flush. "Yeah. Okay. Whatever."

He kissed her lightly on the lips, taking an extra second, simply because he could.

"What was that for?" Rani asked, slightly breathless.

"Insurance." He laughed as the children whooped at them. "If children believe you, you're golden."

Rani shook her head at him. "Well, okay then. But you do not have to buy a ring because the children say so."

"All right. Back to work. Get back on stage. Dr. Rani is going to take you through 'Hakuna Matata.'" Param made shooing motions and the children backed up and went to work.

He pulled out his phone and texted his brothers. Need to buy Rani a ring.

The responses were immediate.

Nishant: You haven't bought her a ring yet? What's the matter with you?

Milan: Seems if you look like garam-garam Param, you can get a woman to marry you without even giving her a ring.

He shook his head at his brothers and pocketed his phone. His lips were still buzzing from Rani's kiss.

"Hey. Your favorite today, Mug and bhakri," Param said as he laid out the food at the clinic later that night.

"You really are the best." She reached for one of the flatbreads while he nuked the lentil soup. She meant it. Param's cooking kept her from eating out of the vending machines.

"That's why you're marrying me," he said slightly louder than necessary, so the staff could hear.

Rani rolled her eyes. "As long as the food keeps coming after we're married," she answered equally loud and with a smirk.

"You got it, sweetheart," Param said and kissed her forehead.

He passed her a bowl of the lentil soup and another bhakri and sat down next to her.

"The kids are disgusted that I'm marrying my best friend." He chuckled.

"It is kind of gross," Rani agreed. "If you're twelve."

"And if you're not twelve?"

"It's not quite as gross," she said as she popped a piece of bhakri into her mouth, avoiding his gaze for the moment. The thought of really marrying her best friend was not gross at all. "Especially if you're faking," she whispered, catching his eye. The moment was like so many others that they'd shared over the years, conspiratorial, a secret between only the two of them. It was also the reason she would never *actually* marry her best friend. She would not want to lose these moments. They were too precious to her.

"That is the best part," he agreed. "Because when we divorce, we'll absolutely still be friends."

"It's perfect." Rani grinned, the way she only grinned at him and at no one else. "The best of both worlds. We should have thought of this sooner. My dad is telling everyone that I'm no longer available. And when we get divorced, I can ride that for at least another year."

"So you don't ever want to get married?" he asked.

"No." Rani frowned as she spooned mug into her mouth. "You know this."

He shook his head. "We have never had this conversation. I'm surprised. Your parents were very happy."

"Well, that's it, isn't it?" she said as she scooped more mug onto her spoon.

"What?"

"My parents were very happy, in love, three kids, a practice, the whole thing. Then she died, and my dad was destroyed. He couldn't even take care of his children." Rani picked at her bhakri without eating it. "He lost himself to my mom, and vice versa. It was like they couldn't live without one another. That may sound romantic, but I watched my dad really not be able to function without her." She paused to chew. "But the flip side is that their marriage was strong because they gave themselves over to one another."

"What about Jason Duvall?"

"Mmm." Rani nodded. "We were together five months. I met his parents, remember?"

Param nodded. "Yes. Then you told him he was distracting you from studying for the MCAT and you broke up."

"Yes."

"Deep Kulkarni. I was convinced you were going marry him," Param recalled. He hated the guy. Even the fact that he was Milan's neurologist didn't change the fact that Param just did not like the man.

"You hated him." Rani laughed. "But yes." Her voice got soft. "I thought about marriage with him—for a hot second. We were together for eight months in med school—like a lifetime at the time."

"You never said what happened." Param leaned toward her.

Rani started eating again. "He just wasn't right for me. Too…smooth or something." She shrugged. "I don't know. Karina says it's because I'm afraid to commit."

She looked like she was going to say something more, but she did not.

"Are you afraid? To commit?" Param watched her closely.

"Maybe. I know I'm afraid of losing the person I give my heart and soul to. My mom and dad gave themselves over to each other. When she…was gone, my dad was lost. To a certain degree he stayed that way. I'm not willing let the same thing happen to me." She watched Param watch her for a moment. She could have acted on her high school crush on him all those years ago, but there was a part of her that had always been afraid of loving him too much and then possibly losing him.

"So, you're never going to really give your heart and soul to anyone?" Param mused.

She nodded and shook her head. "Karina says… never mind."

"What does Karina say?" Param leaned toward her.

She eyed him for a minute as she considered whether or not to tell him. "Karina says that's the reason I'm okay to marry you. Because I've already made a commitment to you." She sighed. "But the jokes on her. Since you and I are not in a real relationship."

Something flashed across his face, but it was gone before Rani could discern what it was. "No." His smile looked forced. "I suppose not." He sat back and watched her a moment. "Though we are quite the pair. I find myself unable to trust my own judgment when it comes to women."

"Like who?"

"Angelina Vasquez."

Rani rolled her eyes to mask the flood of jealousy that washed over her. "I knew you liked her."

"That's just it. I should like her. Smart, great with kids, beautiful and she's interested in me." He paused. "Well, she's pissed at me now, but she was interested."

"But…" Rani leaned toward him now.

"But I feel…nothing." He looked her in the eye. "Truth?"

"Always."

"Even with Sangeeta—there wasn't that…spark." He said softly.

"Spark?" She knew what he was talking about, because she had felt it.

With him.

"Well, then good thing she bolted, huh?"

He turned to his food, picking at the bhakhri, shaking his head. "Just say it like it is, Rani."

"Sorry."

"You are not."

"True."

They sat in silence for a moment. Then Param leaned in and whispered, "In any case. I'm very grateful to you for helping me out with this whole fiasco to help Milan. I knew I could count on you."

"Always." Rani reached out and squeezed his hand. They really did not do the touchy feely kind of thing, but they'd been touching each other more lately and she didn't hate it. "We've been looking out for Milan together for a long time."

He moved his hand away and stood. Rani immediately felt the absence of his body beside hers.

"I should go. You must have patients."

Rani stood to wash her hands. "Thanks again for the food."

"Thanks for volunteering to read seventh-grade English papers."

"I didn't volunteer for that." Rani furrowed her brow.

Param smirked at her as he walked out the door. "Yes. You did. When you agreed to marry me."

Chapter Twenty-Five

Honestly, if Param Sheth was not her best friend, she'd be inclined to punch him in the mouth. Check that. Forget the fact that he's her best friend. She still wanted to punch him in the mouth.

Her phone buzzed. Another text from Param. He had made plans for them without asking her. Plans that involved another couple. And he would not give her the details.

She could feel him smirking through the texts.

She stomped into her house still fuming. She'd had the day from hell. Not the patients, but all the red tape around taking care of those precious little people. Why did admin make it so hard to care for children?

"What?" Param said as soon as he saw her face. "You're still mad?" He raised his eyebrows, as if completely shocked.

He was here? Of course he was here. He was always everywhere.

"Are we still double dating with…whoever?" she barked.

Param walked closer to her and whispered loudly, "Yes. We are a couple. It's what couples do."

"Not me."

"It's a night out. We'll go for drinks and then a concert." Param made it sound like she should be excited about this.

"I have to talk to people I don't know," she grumbled.

"You do that every day, for work," he said, narrowing his eyes.

"Exactly," she growled. It took all her energy to be "on" at work for the children and their either helicopter or negligent parents. When she got home, all she wanted was to snuggle up on the sofa with her fiancé and watch a movie.

Wait. No. She wanted to snuggle up with a book. She didn't really have a fiancé.

She barely registered the surprised and hurt look on his face when Sona came in.

"Perfect, you're both here," Sona said cheerily. Sona was the resident extrovert, while Rani enveloped herself in the introvert label like it was a cozy blanket. Sona handed each of them a garment bag of clothes. "Go get changed."

"For what?" Rani did not want anything right now but the warmth and comfort of her bed. Maybe some kulfi.

Sona grinned from ear to ear. "Surprise!"

Panic flooded through Rani. "A party?" She was still recovering from the "impromptu" engagement party

Veena Auntie had thrown them. Hadn't they had enough parties?

"No, silly." Sona laughed. "Wedding photo shoot! By yours truly."

It was a fact that Sona was an excellent photographer. She had an eye for things none of them saw. And as such, Rani had agreed to letting her take a few photos at their "wedding." She had not agreed to whatever Sona thought was happening right now.

"We never asked for a photo shoot," said Rani as she shifted her gaze to Param.

"Sona texted me to come over after school." He held his hands out and shook his head. He'd had no more idea about this than she did.

"Hence the surprise." Sona spoke like Rani was the idiot here.

"Where?" She looked around the house. No sign of lights or those umbrella things Sona used.

"I set up in the backyard."

"It's February. In Maryland. There's snow on the ground!" Rani was nearly shouting.

"Exactly. It's just a sprinkling and it will add an aura of romance!" Sona was close to giddy.

"It's cold."

"No worries. I'll be quick. And I borrowed a couple of heaters from the neighbors." She grinned. "I ended up inviting them to the wedding, because it was so awkward borrowing the heaters, but them being right next door, and not being invited."

Rani just stared at her sister, then shifted her glare to Param. "This is your fault." She wasn't sure how it was his fault, but it felt good to vent it out.

He opened his mouth to protest, but Rani cut him off.

"You know why," Rani said, narrowing her eyes.

Param rolled his eyes. "Seriously? We both thought it was a good idea for Sona to take our pictures."

"Fine. But the double date is all your fault."

"Aw…you're going on a double date?" Sona clapped her hands together and sighed. "So cute."

"It's not cute," Rani snapped.

"Okay." Sona acted as if everything was fine. "Just go change and then we'll go get some gorgeous photos."

Rani grabbed her garment bag and headed upstairs to her room. Param followed right behind her.

"What are you doing?" She glared at him halfway up the steps.

"I'm changing like Sona said."

"Not in my room, you're not."

"What's the big deal, Rani?" Sona giggled. "It's not like you haven't seen each other naked. Plus, you might need zipper help."

Rani glared at Param again like it was his fault Sona was talking about being naked. She did not need to be thinking about his big muscular body all naked and everything. Param for his part managed to flush a deep red. Huh. Rani hadn't thought that brown people could manage that shade of red. Turns out they can.

"Oh…uh. I'm good here," Param stuttered, wide-eyed.

"Just go upstairs," Sona insisted. "She's just irritable because she's on her period or something."

"I am not on my period," Rani snapped at her sister, before she turned and made her way up the steps.

Param glared at Rani as he followed her up to her room. She went inside and shut the door as he was walking in. "Are you listening to her?"

"I need to change for the photo shoot," he grumbled.

Rani inhaled deeply. "Fine. But that's your side." She pointed to the side of the room opposite her. Her side had the long mirror.

Param rolled his eyes. "Whatever."

Rani opened the garment bag to find a beautiful baby blue Anarkali dress in a gorgeous flowy silk, with a sheer dupatta. The gown would be fitted through her waist, then flare at the bottom. It was sleeveless and had small mirrors and beads sewn in to add sparkle. She had no idea where Sona might have gotten such an item, but it was gorgeous.

She took it out and laid it on the bed. Param had done the same with his outfit. It was a jabho and tight pants in navy blue, with baby blue threaded detailing throughout and a baby blue scarf. Simple elegance. Say what you want about Sona, but the girl had great taste.

Rani glared at Param. "Turn around."

"Duh," he said, seemingly unable to come up with a better response.

He turned around and she turned and faced the long mirror, quickly removing her scrubs. "I can't believe you made plans for us without consulting me."

"Are you serious?" he barked at her. "We've made plans for each other before."

She peeked over her shoulder to grab her outfit. She caught a quick glance of the back of Param in nothing but his underwear (fitted boxers) pulling up the jabho pants. Damn but the man was beautiful. Bronzed shoulders with muscle bulging out *everywhere*, tapered narrow waist and—Rani had to swallow—a very nice ass atop equally muscular legs. How was she just noticing this now? He started to turn so she quickly turned back and pulled the dress over her head. The image of his bronzed body seemed imprinted to the insides of her eyelids.

"But not as a couple. You're supposed to be my best friend, but it's like you don't even know me." The zipper was a side zip, and Rani managed it, but not before catching some of her skin in it. The zipper drew a small dot of blood.

"Damn it." She swiped at the blood, but it kept coming.

"How did you manage to make yourself bleed?" he asked as he approached her with a tissue. At least his bottoms were on, but he was shirtless. He pressed the tissue into her side to stop the bleeding. She snuck a glance at him in the mirror, only to find him looking at her. She looked away. Or at least she tried to. How was a girl supposed to look away from a shirtless Param Sheth while he was tending to her?

"Um, okay. I think it's stopped." Param pulled up the zipper, his fingers gently grazing her side. She was immediately transported to the last time his fingers had grazed her skin in that exact spot. Her tongue had been in his mouth, and his fingers had inched under her crop top.

She held her breath, unable to stop watching him in the mirror, unable to stop the electric current that zinged through her from his fingers to everywhere else in her body.

His fingers shook as he fastened the zipper then caught her eye in the mirror.

"I guess your sister was right, you did need zipper help." He went back to his side.

She was speechless. She brushed out her hair and

swiped on some mascara and lip gloss. She knew Sona would just send her back up if she didn't.

"I am your best friend. And I do know you," he finally said.

She turned to face him and lost her breath in her chest somewhere. Param half naked had been a sight to behold, but Param in that outfit was…breathtaking. The deep navy of the jabho complemented his skin, and the cut was perfect. The soft material hugged his shoulders and upper arms, grazing his chest and back. He had rolled up the sleeves, exposing strong, corded forearms. It wasn't the first time Rani had seen Param dressed like this, but it was the first time he made her breath catch.

Or was it?

Param raked his gaze up and down her fitted, A-line outfit with such intensity, she swore she could feel it.

"We should go," Rani snapped, more harshly than she intended.

"Fine." Param extended his arm for her to lead the way.

"Fine." She bustled past him and down the stairs where Sona waited patiently.

"Oh my god! I knew you two would look amazing in these outfits!" She grabbed her camera. "Come on. This won't take long."

Sona had her light all set up in the backyard. The dusting of about an inch of snow did add romance to the setting. Rani inhaled and tried not to think about the level of documentation that was going into her fake wedding.

Sona had them do a few classic poses, with Rani in front and Param behind her with his arms around her.

Then side by side, etc. Then she asked them to walk around hand in hand, and talk and look at each other.

"Hello."

Rani froze with Param's hand in hers. Patel Dada. *Don't look at Param. Don't look at Param.* She looked at him. He had the same look of panic on his face that she felt in her heart that was probably on her face, because she could never hide her feelings anyway.

"Oh, hi, Patel Dada. Glad you could make it," Sona said brightly. "Could you stand over there? Something is not right." Sona adjusted the lights and took a few more shots.

"Where are you taking my sister tonight?" Sona asked Param from behind the lens.

"Um, to a concert," Param answered. "Hi, Patel Dada."

"Ignore him," Sona commanded. "Focus on your fiancée."

"With people," Rani added.

"Yes, Rani. People are usually present at concerts," Param murmured, his patience with her was waning.

"Can you two face each other?" Sona asked.

They complied. Rani tried not to roll her eyes. She might have failed. "I know people are at concerts. You didn't even ask me," she murmured back.

"Move closer to each other."

They did so, but it was as if they were nine years old and the other one had cooties.

"I don't care that you're mad at him, Rani," Sona called out. "Move closer."

She inched closer to him.

"Closer," Sona demanded. "Like your bodies almost touching."

Rani did as she was told. It was cold out, and Param

was giving off some intense heat, so being close to him felt good. Really good.

"Put your hand on her face," Sona directed. "And look at her."

Param gently rested a warm hand on her face.

"Rani, lift your chin so you're looking at him." Sona was in the zone.

Rani lifted her chin with Param's hand still on her cheek and looked up at him. Her eyes met his, and all the annoyance was gone from them. Instead, his eyes were soft. Her gaze drifted over his mouth. A sense of longing she had never experienced overcame her as she focused in on Param's lips. She been there before, and she wanted nothing more than to lose herself there again.

"Param, lean down like you're going to kiss her."

Yes! Please!

Param leaned down and Rani reflexively lifted her mouth toward his in anticipation of his lips finally on hers. Of the sweet bliss of escape she found in his arms. Their bodies were, in fact, touching and their hearts beat rapidly. Rani could not distinguish her heartbeat from his. His breath was on her mouth, just a little nudge and she would be kissing Param.

Again. This would be the third time. Or was it the fourth. She had lost count. Why was she counting anyway, they were supposed to be engaged, they should be all over each all the time, there was no need to count kisses.

Except that she was.

"That's perfect," Sona called before they actually kissed. "Hold it right there. Perfect, got it. It's the almost kiss that makes the best picture. You two are free to go to see One Republic."

Rani took a step back before she realized what Sona had said. "What?" She looked at Param, who was looking irritated at Sona now. "We're going to see One Republic?" They were her most favorite band of all time and she had never seen them in concert. "Ohh!" she squealed. "That means Milan and Aisha are coming with us. They're the 'couple,' right?" She completely forgot that Patel Dada was there watching the whole thing.

"Surprise!" Param said, doing lame jazz hands since he hadn't gotten to actually surprise her.

"That is the best surprise ever!" Rani jumped up and hugged him. She noted that he hesitated a fraction of a second before hugging her back. "Why the surprise?"

Sona rolled her eyes. "Rani, seriously? It's Valentine's Day."

"Oh! Is it?" She turned to Param. "But we—" she passed a finger back and forth between them "—don't do that."

"I was trying to be a good fiancé." He widened his eyes at her and nodded, reminding her of their ruse and Patel Dada still watching them.

"Right." She lay a hand on his chest. His heart was still racing as fast as hers. He was warm and strong and in that moment she wished he was really hers. "And you are a good fiancé."

"Aww, that last pose will make a great announcement pic." Sona had been still taking shots. "Sometimes, the candids are the best. I'll send them to you as soon as I edit them."

Right. The announcement for their real wedding of their fake relationship.

"So, Rani, you seemed irritated with Param," Patel Dada said as he approached them.

"Well, he made plans for me without telling me."

"Surprise plans. For Valentine's Day," Param said.

"Which we don't do," Rani countered.

"So you don't want to go see One Republic?" Param asked

"Of course I do."

"So what's the problem?" Param looked at Patel Dada for assistance.

Patel Dada chuckled and raised his hands. "I have no idea what has happened here. She sounds like my wife. Though I appreciate the reminder. I should go and get her something." He looked at them both, his expression unreadable. "Enjoy your evening."

Param followed Rani into the house and up to her room. His clothes were in there, after all. He could still feel Rani's cool hands on his face, and her breath on his lips. Silence stretched between them as they walked up the stairs.

Once in the room, Param went to his corner and quickly removed the jabho, replacing it with the long-sleeved T-shirt he'd had on earlier. Rani was still dressed and trying to undo the side zipper that was located on her waist but under her arm, making it difficult to access. Her back was to him.

He walked over and placed his hand on hers and tried the zipper again. She was standing in front of the mirror and saw his reflection. He looked at her in the mirror and nodded toward the zipper. She removed her hand. He tugged gently at the zipper and it slid down effortlessly. He glanced in the mirror and found her looking at him. The thought visited him that he could simply lift the dress over her head and he would be able to touch as much of her skin as he wanted. Or he could move her hair aside and kiss the side of her neck. Funny, she was his best friend, but he had no idea how soft the skin on her neck might be. He imagined the rest of her body was as soft and strong as her hands. His heart pounded in his chest and he moved on instinct, not listening to any voice of reason. Her hair was thick, soft silk when he moved it aside to expose her neck. His fingers grazed the delicate skin under her hair, causing goosebumps to come up. It was heady, to realize that he affected Rani that way. She watched him in the mirror as he rested a hand in the softness of her hair and bent his head toward her neck, inhaling her scent—something citrusy, but also a hint of disinfectant from the hospital. He wanted her. He wanted Rani. He met her eyes in the mirror as his lips grazed her neck. *His Rani.*

"Just hang the clothes and I'll grab them tomorrow," Sona called up.

Param startled and released the dress, her hair, and Rani, stepping back from her. "There's no neck hook," he announced to her.

"Okay," Rani called. She avoided his gaze and turned back to the mirror.

He went back to his corner, and quickly changed pants. By the time he turned back around, Rani had donned jeans and a sweater for the concert.

"Ready?" He looked at his phone. "Milan and Aisha are on their way to get us."

"Yes. Sure. I'm ready." But she didn't make eye contact.

"Rani," he started softly. "I'm—"

"Late. Aren't Milan and Aisha waiting for us?"

He stared at her. "Rani. About what just happened…"

She widened her eyes. "What happened? You helped me unzip my dress. Big deal. We're grown-ups." She gathered her things not looking at him at all. "Let's go."

Param watched her walk out the door. "Okay."

Chapter Twenty-Six

"I swear, Patel Dada is coming to this concert," Rani said for the fiftieth time, looking all around.

"No, he's not. He probably doesn't even know who One Republic is," Param insisted.

"Just in case, I think we should try to get on that big screen kissing," Rani whispered.

"That's only in sports." Param laughed. "We have box seats, courtesy of Milan's work. Patel Dada will not be there," Param said as they walked into the box. "I'm sure of it."

"Patel Dada!" Rani said loudly, as she elbowed him in the ribs. "What a surprise!"

Param swore under his breath as he grabbed his ribs.

"Well, I needed a Valentine's Day gift, and Milan was kind enough to oblige at the last minute." Param shot a look at Milan, who grinned and waved back, completely oblivious to Param's irritation.

"This box is great, right?" Milan said. "Aisha and I DJ'd for this company's Christmas party last year, and now he gets me tickets every so often."

"Of course he does. He needs to keep the best DJ team happy," said Rani.

She was walking around the suite like a child in a candy store. One Republic really was her favorite band. Seeing them in concert was on her bucket list. When Milan had mentioned they were the ones in concert, Param hadn't hesitated. Even at the discount, it was expensive. But he knew it would make her happy.

"This is amazing! Thank you, Milan." She was nearly squealing.

"Oh, don't thank me. This was all Bhai's idea. Your first Valentine's Day as a couple and all."

She raised her eyebrows at Param, and he shrugged. He could feel Patel Dada watching them. She stepped closer to Param and wrapped her arms around him. "This really is amazing."

Param took her hand and led her to the two rows of seats. They walked all the way to the front corner. "From here, you get the best view." She leaned into him and Param realized that he wanted to believe with all his heart that she did so because she wanted to, and not because Patel Dada was lurking around.

"This is…" Her face said it all.

He leaned down and kissed her mouth lightly. "Anything to make you happy."

If she was shocked by his kiss, she did not show it, she simply beamed at him. "Thank you. Best Valentine's Day ever!" They sat down, still holding hands and watched the concert.

Param watched Rani almost the whole time. He had to agree. Best Valentine's Day ever.

Rani was having the best Valentine's Day ever. She had never really celebrated Valentine's Day, convinced it was simply a Hallmark holiday and that it didn't mean anything. But concert tickets to your favorite band from your best friend/fake fiancé were pretty damn awesome.

The fact that Patel Dada was here meant more touching and more kissing in public than she would have liked. Anyone who really knew her would know that if she really were *with* Param, she wouldn't be kissing him in public. It just wasn't her jam.

Param never left her side, unless he was getting her a drink or food. Totally the doting fiancé. It occurred to Rani in that moment that Param would make a great boyfriend, and eventual husband for some lucky woman. Sangeeta Parikh was a complete idiot for running from this man. In that same moment, Rani experienced the strongest wave of jealousy she'd ever experienced. Picturing Param sitting in this box with his arm around another woman, or holding her hand, or even kissing her made her not see green, but see red. She shook her head to remind herself that Param's doting on her was for show, not for real.

"Here you go." Param slipped past where she was sitting and sat down next to her, handing her a gin and tonic. "I got you some food since we didn't have time to eat before we left." He handed her a plate of nachos and settled in with his old-fashioned, pulling her close and kissing her lightly on the lips.

It was a tease. Not two hours ago she had been ready to lose herself in this man's kisses. She knew this moment was for show, but she wanted to believe that it was a lead up to something more.

This is what it would feel like to be Param Sheth's fiancée. Surprise concert tickets, thoughtfulness, kissing and more. When he got married—to someone else—he'd spend his time doting on his wife. Cooking for her. Being a father to their children. There would not be as much room for Rani in that life.

She waited for this flood of jealousy to overcome her as she realized that once this farce was over, Param might very well be ready to date and meet his life partner. But it didn't come. Not because she wouldn't miss him, but because in all those scenarios, he was happy. That was what she wanted for him. She had made her own choices. She knew she would be alone, it was a side effect of not wanting to give yourself over to anyone as completely needed as it was in a marriage.

She watched him watch the concert, a smile on his face, tousled hair that still looked amazing, a slight scruff on his face. Without thinking, she reached out and ran her hand along the roughness. Param turned toward her, a question in his eyes.

"You okay?" he spoke almost directly into her ear, causing goosebumps on that side of her body. Huh. One whisper and her whole body responded.

She smiled and nodded. "Just doing my part."

"Right." He nodded, the smile still on his face, though she thought she might have detected a flicker of disappointment in his voice.

She pulled her hand back and settled once again into his arms to enjoy the concert. This was as close to bliss as she had ever gotten. And it was as close as she would ever get.

But that didn't mean it wasn't nice.

The concert finished, and Milan and Aisha insisted they hang out for a bit longer with them. Neither Param nor Rani wanted to leave, so they stayed. Patel Dada went home after the concert was over. They laughed and talked with Milan and Aisha for a bit. Every so often, Milan would drag Param to a corner and show him something on his phone.

"What is that all about?" Rani asked Aisha.

Aisha grinned at her. "I have no idea."

But the way she said it, Rani felt like she knew exactly what they were doing. It was very late by the time they were done, and Param's apartment was closer than going home.

"Want to just stay over?" Param asked as they got in the car.

"Might as well. I have an early day tomorrow." Rani had already brought scrubs over as she was slowly moving in.

They talked for a few minutes about the concert and how good Milan looked, before they each became lost in their own thoughts. They entered the house and Rani went up to the small guestroom and Param went to his.

Her face wash was in his bathroom so shifted direction and went to his room to retrieve it.

"Thank you for the concert," she said, standing in the doorway of his bedroom after getting her product.

He turned to her. "Of course."

"Sorry I was so mean earlier."

Param shrugged. "Not the first time."

She nodded. "True. Probably not the last."

"Also true." He smiled and shook his head at her.

He was standing not three feet away from her, his long-sleeved T-shirt and old jeans clinging to all parts of his body, just enough to tease, but not enough to satisfy. His hair was tousled from his habit of running his hands through it. That feeling of wanting to lose herself to him returned. Her heart pounded in her chest. "Param?"

"Yes?"

"About what happened earlier today?"

"You yelling at me?" he chuckled. "I'm used to it."

She shook her head and looked him in the eye. "No. Not that."

He snapped his gaze to her. "I'm sorry. Just getting carried away with the role…"

Kiss me. It was on the tip of her tongue. It was all she had thought about all evening. She would surely burst if Param Sheth did not kiss her. *Really kiss her.*

Param was standing there, watching her with those eyes. If she asked, he would kiss her, she knew it. But she couldn't be that selfish.

"Yes. Just carried away." She turned to go.

"Rani…"

"Better get some sleep." She left.

Chapter Twenty-Seven

Rani had left for work by the time he woke the next morning. He hadn't expected to see her, but he hadn't slept all night either. All he had wanted to do last night was kiss Rani senseless. Though it was probably a good idea that he had not done so, because he would not have stopped there. That would have complicated matters plenty.

Or simplified it.

Huh.

Not to mention, his brothers were on him to buy Rani a ring. Nishant had been texting him and Milan pictures of diamond rings all night during and after the concert.

They were coming to get him to make that purchase. Which made him nervous for some reason.

Nishant picked up Milan first, then swung around to get Param. Milan got out of the passenger seat and sat in the back when Param came out. Common knowledge among the brothers that Param's legs needed more room than either of theirs.

"Thanks, Milan," Param said as he sat down.

"Yeah, yeah. Got to make room for the legs and the big head," Milan said from the back seat.

Param turned and bumped the insides of his fists together at him. Which made Milan laugh.

"Listen, you two. I'm a middle-school teacher. Not a hotshot lawyer or an up-and-coming DJ. Don't be taking me to wherever you two bought your rings. Rani's a simple woman," Param told his brothers. Param's first instinct had been to just delay the ring shopping until after they were married, and then divorced.

But then he decided he would like nothing more than to buy Rani a ring. Not an engagement ring. Not a friendship ring—she'd probably throw that right back at him. But a ring that expressed what she meant to him. Something she would want to keep after they were divorced. His stomach sort of knotted every time he thought about divorcing her.

"Hey, hey." Param pointed at the exit. "Don't forget to stop at the hospital. I'm dropping off food for her."

This resulted in the most middle school of behaviors from his brothers. "Aw. You really are the sweetest," Milan chuckled.

"You know she's probably only marrying you for your cooking ability." Nishant smirked. "Couldn't be any other 'ability,' huh, Milan?"

"Well, you certainly can't drop that off." Milan laughed.

Param flushed because of course he and Rani had not slept together, and likely would not. But he was taken back to yesterday, when he had considered finding out what her skin felt like, so now he was thinking about Rani naked. In bed with him.

"He's turning red." Nishant chuckled, looking in the rearview mirror.

"You two are middle schoolers, okay? Actually, no. That's insulting to my students. How about that?" The teacher in him came out. "Middle school boys would be disappointed in your behavior." Param shook his head at them.

Nishant pulled over in the parking lot next to the ED, and Param ran in and dropped off Rani's food at the nurses' station, since she was with patients.

Nishant was no fool, but he did take Param to the exact place he bought Pankthi's ring, which was also where Milan purchased Aisha's ring. It also happened to be where Param had bought Sangeeta's ring. Param recognized it right away. The three of them had done all of the purchases together.

He closed his eyes. "You brought me back here?" He glared at Nishant next to him, and Milan through the rearview mirror. "Not to mention that I just told you I have a budget, not twenty minutes ago?" Param said, still seated in the car.

"Can you just trust me?" Nishant turned to him. "Yes, it's the same place, because they know our family and will honestly respect your budget."

Param stared ahead at the jewelry store, which was a family owned business in a small strip mall. It was currently run by the original owner children, Shaylin and Ami. This was the place his father bought his mom gifts. Both brothers had purchased engagement rings and wedding bands here. Shaylin and his family were more than fair. They never nickeled and dimed, always more concerned about whether you were happy with your purchase.

"They're invited to your wedding," Milan offered.

Param snapped his head around. "Seriously?"

Both brothers shrugged. They didn't control the invite list.

"It's embarrassing," Param said.

"Get over it," they said in unison, then high-fived each other for doing so.

"But, Bhai, seriously. We love Rani. She's like a sister to us. We want her to have the best," Milan started. "This place is the best. Who cares if it's your second time around? This time will stick."

"One hundred percent," agreed Nishant.

Param had to look away from his brothers. This was not going to stick. He already knew that. But these two pains in the ass were his people. He hated lying to them even if it was for Milan's own good. In a perfect world, he would have dragged them out here to get the ring before he proposed to Rani. The world wasn't perfect, and neither were he and his brothers, but he loved them to death all the same. They did truly love Rani and wanted to make sure that he did right by her.

"Just swing your giraffe legs out of the car and come on," demanded Milan. "It took you this long to put a ring on it, the least you could do is make it a good ring."

Param extricated himself from Nishant's sedan. His brothers were shivering in the bitter cold, so the three of them quickly entered the small family-owned jewelry store.

"Well, if it isn't Nishant Sheth and brothers," an attractive young woman greeted them. Shaylin's sister, Ami, Param recalled.

"Hey, Ami," Nishant said as he extended his hand in greeting. "You remember Milan and Param?" He motioned to them.

"Sure do." She looked right at Milan. "Round cut. 1.25 carat, good quality on a platinum band."

"You got it." Milan chuckled.

She turned to Param and paused. "Ready to give it another try?"

Param flushed. "I am."

"Don't worry about it. It happens more than you'd think." Ami shrugged at the shocked expression on his face. "Just getting all the elephants out of the room, you know? That way we can look for the right ring for this very lucky woman without all the other stuff invading our minds." She paused and looked at each of them in turn. She was five feet tall without heels, but she held them in her gaze with the power of her presence. "Make sense?"

The three of them nodded as if being directed by a teacher.

The store was small by any standard, just one case in a U-shape. The case housed samples, ideas, because they didn't stock very much. Why stock when everything was custom-made?

Ami was about their age. Her father had started the business thirty-plus years ago. He still did the design and such, but Shaylin and Ami pretty much ran things now.

"First of all, I'm going to get Shaylin to bring out some glasses and that bottle of Macallan he hides, and we are going to toast you, and wish you luck on that upcoming proposal," Ami told them. "Shaylin," she called out. "Bring the Macallan and five glasses."

"Sure thing," a voice called from the back. Within minutes, Shaylin arrived holding the goods.

"I already proposed," Param told her. Which he in fact did not do, come to think of it.

"What?" Shaylin stopped in the middle of pouring to look at his brothers.

They both shrugged. "Apparently, if you look like that—" Nishant waved his hand over Param "—you don't need a ring."

"Shut up." Param shook his head, feeling his face flush. "It's not my fault all the good-looking genes came my way." He chuckled. "Blame Mom and Dad." He was then forced to dodge the gloves and hats that his brothers threw at him.

"Wait, she said yes?" Shaylin somehow found this hard to believe.

Param nodded.

"Oh, so you're scoping things out, and she'll come pick out her own ring," Shaylin said.

"No. I'm buying a ring tonight. It's a surprise."

"Of course you are," Ami said. "Just because she said yes does not mean she doesn't want a ring."

They toasted Param and then Ami pulled out the diamonds.

"So Ami." Param sidled closer to the young woman. "I have a budget…" Param gave her a number.

Ami smiled warmly. "I am aware, Mr. English teacher. Don't you worry, I will make sure you'll find the perfect thing for her." She stood back and shook her head. "That's not to say that you shouldn't get paid way better than whatever you're getting right now."

The five of them spent the next couple hours looking at diamonds and settings, until one of the combinations hit. Param closed his eyes for a moment. When he opened them, he let himself believe he was really buying Rani an engagement ring.

Param had known what he wanted once he finally saw it. A simple gold band, with a flush setting for a single diamond. It was perfect, it wouldn't rip her gloves when she wore it to work, and it was beautiful without all the glitz and glamour, just like the woman who would wear it.

And just a tad outside his budget. But Param could make it happen for Rani.

"Just get the wedding band, too," Nishant advised quietly. "You'll get a good deal here."

Param closed his eyes and sighed. He nodded, and then selected the perfect wedding band to go with the engagement ring. Rani was going to love this.

Too bad she was going to give it back to him.

"Dr. Mistry, there's someone here to see you." One of the nurses cracked open the door to the dark and empty doctor's lounge where Rani was trying to sleep on the sofa.

Rani needed the sleep, but she hadn't heard from Param all day. "Tell Param to come on back."

"It's not Param, although he left food for you at the nurses' station."

Rani's heart plummeted. Param always ate with her. She couldn't remember a time that he hadn't. And she had been looking forward to seeing him. Rani groaned. "Then tell whoever it is that I'm sleeping. And don't eat my food."

"You don't want me to, trust me," the young man spoke in a hushed tone. "It's Dr. Kulkarni."

Rani bolted upright. No! Was something up with Milan? "Is it about a patient? I'll be there in a minute."

"It's fine. I'm here." His voice hit her, smooth and deep like silk.

"Deep?" she said, flicking on the light. "You caught me napping. Is something wrong with Milan? I didn't think he had anything scheduled."

"No. It's nothing like that." Deep seemed a bit tense. He stared at her.

She had just been lying down on her ponytail, so her hair was for sure sticking up. She never wore makeup on shift, so there was that. So basically, she was standing there with bedhead and bags under her eyes talking to Deep Kulkarni.

"I heard via the grapevine that you're trying to get funding for a pediatric free clinic," Deep said as he entered the lounge.

"I am." She sighed and sat back down on the sofa. She yawned. "Sorry. It's slow going. Red tape and whatnot."

"Dr. Mistry. Incoming," the nurse called out to her from behind Deep.

"I'll be right there, Marc," Rani said as she stood and fixed her ponytail.

"Listen, my dad holds these fundraiser gala events for all the deep pockets he knows. If you have an elevator pitch, I can get you in…" He shrugged.

"Wait." Rani froze mid-ponytail-fixing. "Are you serious? Because it's a really bad joke."

Deep laughed. "I'm serious. I know how you feel about pediatrics, I would not make this up."

She grinned. This could be a huge step toward a

proper clinic. "If you can get me in, I would totally owe you one, Deep."

"I can get you in. And it would be my pleasure." Deep grinned at her and chuckled. "I've missed your energy and passion."

"Dr. Mistry," Marc came back.

"On my way." Rani nearly ran to the door. "Text me the details. Thank you so much."

Chapter Twenty-Eight

The door opened and Nishant let himself into Param's house. He brought the cold air with him. Param had just returned from dropping off mug and rice for Rani and had started the dishes.

"Hey." Nishant toed off his shoes and hung his coat on the hook by the door. He entered and helped himself to a beer.

"Hey."

Nishant looked over Param's shoulder at the tiffin he was washing. "Where were you?"

"Hospital."

Nishant nodded. "Dropping off food for your 'fiancée.'" He used the air quotes.

"Why the air quotes?" Param asked as he scrubbed the liner of his Instant Pot.

"Because I know for a fact that you two are faking." Nishant paused. "Or at least she is."

Param turned away from Nishant and concentrated on washing his pot. "We're getting married." Stick with the story. "Not to mention, you watched me buy her an engagement ring and a wedding band."

"Uh-huh. There is that. And I'm all for it." He leaned against the small granite counter. "Remember a few years ago, Rani was dating that guy in med school?"

"Deep Kulkarni, Milan's neuro?" Param had never liked Deep. Too smooth. Walked around throwing his money around. He had really only liked how Rani looked on his arm. He was the closest Rani had ever gotten to marrying someone.

"Well, yeah, him. But I meant the other one. Blond hair, played the guitar."

"Jason." Param liked him better than Deep. At least he was down to earth. Rani broke up with him, too. Said he had no ambition.

Nishant snapped his fingers. "Yes. Well, we had all gone out together, the first time we met him and re-member none of us even realized they were a couple, except you."

"She had told me." She told him almost everything.

"Right. But we didn't even clue in on it because they didn't so much as hold hands or even sit together." He paused. He looked back at Param.

Param continued doing the dishes. He still had pa-pers to grade and he needed to get this done. "Rani doesn't do PDA. Like ever. She doesn't want the world to know her business."

Nishant grinned and nodded his head. "Rani doesn't do PDA. You had told me at that time."

"So?"

"So… Aisha told Pankthi how cute you two were at

that concert on Valentine's Day. Even with Patel Dada there. All cuddly and affectionate." Nishant stared at him. "At the engagement party, you two were kissing in front of all the guests. Sure *you* do PDA, but Rani… does not. If Rani is going out of her way to show PDA, she's making a point."

"Nishant…" He did not want to talk about this.

"Talk to me, little brother," Nishant said softly. "I thought when you bought the rings…but when I spoke to Pankthi last night…"

Param stared at his big brother. The guy he'd looked up to as a kid, the one who'd had his back. Param shut off the water and dried his hands, tossing the towel onto the counter as if it had done him wrong.

"Rani and I have looked out for Milan all our lives. Our friendship started because she was there for one of Milan's seizures when I was in detention."

"We all know the story. And how much both of you care for Milan," Nishant agreed.

Param placed his hands on the counter and leaned on his arms. "We wanted to help Milan. We already know each other so well, it made sense to pretend we were a couple and get married to unlock Dadaji's trust." Param shrugged and looked away from his brother. He really was an idiot.

"But?"

"No but. That's it." Param was done with this conversation. There couldn't be any more.

"You fell for her for real," Nishant said.

Param worked his jaw and stared at his big brother. He could not be in love with Rani for real. It would never work. Fear gripped his stomach. Denial. It was the best strategy.

If he convinced Nishant, he could convince himself. "What do I know? I thought I loved Sangeeta, remember?" Param asked. He really had thought he loved her. More than that, he had believed that she loved him. When she ran, he was convinced that he would not ever get his happily-ever-after. How could he, when he had no way of recognizing true love?

"You know plenty. Sangeeta was... I don't know... but that does not define you. You know who you are, Param. Trust your feelings. You and Rani have a lot of history."

"Exactly. I can't be in love with her, Bhai. What if I screw it up? I couldn't take it if I lost her for good." His heart ached at the thought of Rani not being in his life. What would his life even look like without her in it? No. He would rather keep her as a friend than risk loving her and losing her like Sangeeta.

"Can you watch her marry someone else?" Nishant with the hard-hitting questions here.

Param snapped his gaze to his brother. Just the thought nauseated him. "What do you know?"

Nishant chuckled and put his hands up. "Nothing, brother. Nothing. But I'll take that as a no."

"Is this funny to you? Don't be ridiculous."

"Param Sheth. You cook and take food to her at the hospital, at the clinic. You have a room set up for her in your house. You talk to her every day."

"That's what best friends do," Param insisted.

"No. It's not. It's what people do when they're in love."

"I was going to get married. I really thought Sangeeta was The One, but then she left. On our wedding day, no less. If that doesn't say loser, I don't know what does. How could I have been so blind?"

"Thank god Sangeeta Parikh has more sense than you." Nishant waved an arm in the air to make his point. "You are different from me and Milan."

"Seriously, Nishant, are we going down—"

"Hear me out, little brother," Nishant said quietly. Param stared at him a minute before nodding.

"You're different because you lead with your heart. In every situation, you lay everything out. You're all in, all the time. You were like that when we were kids, and you're like that now. You did everything for Milan as a child, and when Rani needed someone, it was you. No limits to what you did for her. You were the same with Sangeeta."

"A lot of good it did me."

"It's who you are. You are the best of the three of us. But you're also the most vulnerable, so you get hurt."

Param nodded, his heart sinking.

"But this time," Nishant shook his head, "this time with Rani, this is right. You can feel it, you just don't trust it because you've been burned."

"If I tell her how I feel, she may bolt. And I'll lose the most important person in my life."

"Or," Nishant looked him hard in the eye, "she'll confess that she loves you too, and you'll have the happiness you deserve."

Chapter Twenty-Nine

Rani walked into Param's house with a few more boxes from her dad's. "Hello?" she called out. "New roommate alert."

"In my office," Param called out.

Rani left her boxes in the small hallway and went up to his office. It was the third bedroom upstairs, right next to the small guest room, which was big enough for a queen bed and not much more. Param had taken time to fix up his office, with a nice desk, a library wall and a gorgeous plush rug.

"Thanks for the mug and rice yesterday. Though that was two meals you dropped off and didn't stay." Rani looked him in the eye. "Everything okay?" Truth was she had missed him. So today, she packed some random things in a box and came over. Not that she needed an excuse to see her best friend.

He lifted his head up from his papers and immediately smiled at her. "I am being drowned by homework I assigned."

"Need some help?"

"Seriously?" He eyed her with trepidation, but there was some hope.

"You said it was part of being married to you," she teased.

"Sit down." He handed her a small stack and a red pen.

She grabbed a chair. "You were not messing around."

"I never joke about grading papers."

Rani widened her eyes and got to work. They worked in companionable silence for a bit. Then she remembered what she had wanted to share with him. "So, guess what?" She continued without waiting for him to guess. "Deep came by to invite me to one of his dad's fundraiser galas. He said it would give me the opportunity to pitch to people who might be interested in donating money to the clinic! Isn't that fabulous? I was hoping you could help me with the pitch."

"Rani." Param shook his head and glanced at her. "He just wants to date you again. That's just an excuse."

"No. He was serious about the invite and the pitching, the whole thing."

"Yes, I'm sure he's serious about getting you back in his bed," Param said, going back to his papers.

"So what?" Rani snapped back. This was not the reaction she had expected. "I'm a grown woman. I can handle myself. And if I get funding for the clinic—"

"So what?" Param put his papers down and glared at her. "You're my fiancée. And you're going to be my wife in like a week. *My wife*. That means no boyfriends."

"He's not my boyfriend, and anyway, I'll be your

fake wife," Rani shot back at him. "And we're not making anything work—it's *fake*!"

"Whatever. I don't think it's a good idea."

"It's for the clinic." Rani was angry.

"Maybe for you it is," Param snapped out at her.

"Why are you so mad? You and I aren't really together," Rani said. "So what if I go out and have a nice time with Deep. We used to have fun together."

"Until he wanted more, and then you ditched him," Param reminded her.

"What's it to you, anyway. I'd never let Milan down. You and I will get 'married.'" She used the air quotes and his face hardened.

"Because I don't like seeing my best friend continually putting herself in the same bad situations over and over and then I have to pick up the pieces!" Param was shouting now. He *never* shouted.

"Who picked up the pieces when you were dumped after dating a woman for two years?" Rani stood and shouted right back. She shouted routinely.

"That is low." Param narrowed his eyes at her as he stood. "And said by the woman who chose a career that requires no commitment. Treat them and turf them. Take care of what they need in the moment, but don't get attached to anyone."

She narrowed her eyes at him. Now who was being low? "What about you? *Dragging* me on your honeymoon because you couldn't stand to be alone!"

"Oh, I dragged you?" He shook his head.

"Well, god forbid you deal with any part of your life without me to hold your hand," Rani shot back. She was just being mean now. But she couldn't stop. Param was literally the most frustrating man on the planet.

"That's not all that happened on that honeymoon." Param stepped toward her. She was leaning with her bottom against the desk. Param was in front of Rani, and he placed one hand on either side of her as he leaned toward her, his hands on the desk "Was it?" He was working his jaw and there was a heat in his eyes she'd never seen before.

"Wh-what?" She swallowed hard. He was so close. Param had his arms on either side of her, caging her in. Param never—*never*—intentionally used his size to intimidate or overpower. He wasn't right now either, but she was enveloped by him, his body completely surrounding hers.

She liked it.

A lot.

She was pissed at him and she could see the pain in his face. They'd never had a fight like this before. Her breath was coming hard, and so was his. She could swear he could hear her heart thudding in her chest.

"Things happened on that trip, Rani. Things that you never want to discuss. That's okay. Because I. Am. Done. Talking." With that he closed the inch of space between them and everything happened slowly but all at once. His breath mingled with hers and he put his mouth on hers with a fierceness and longing that took her breath away. She pressed into him almost instantly, reckless with need.

She responded without thought. Her body moved as if separated from her mind, but all her mind was registering was that this was *Param*—and she wanted him.

He kissed her nearly senseless, then pulled her legs around his waist, put his large hands on her bottom and picked her up. He knelt down on the carpet, still holding her, still kissing her and lay her down. Guess those muscles were useful for something.

"Rani…"

"Uh-huh. Yes." She threaded her fingers through his hair and kissed him again.

"We've waited long enough for this," Param spoke low in his throat.

"Yes. Yes." She definitely had waited too long.

He chuckled. "Doc has no words."

"No. Words." All she had was sensation. "Stop talking."

He leaned over her and she put her mouth on his. Every second she wasn't kissing him was a waste of time. When she pulled back to breathe, she grabbed the ends of his T-shirt and tugged. He had the shirt off in a second. She gently dragged her fingers over his chest and shoulders. His eyes rolled into the back of his head as he groaned. He reached his hand under her shirt to the skin of her waist and kissed her again.

"I knew your skin would be super soft," he mumbled as he drew his hands over her belly, scrunching the T-shirt from inside and then pulling it over her head.

She'd never felt so safe and cherished in all her life.

"Rani—"

"Stop. Talking. Just kiss me again." She grinned at him. "And Param?"

"Yes." He hovered over her, his chest just grazing hers, deliciously agonizing, as that scant space was electrified with heat.

"Don't stop."

Chapter Thirty

He did not stop. For that matter, neither did she. Everything he'd ever felt for her surfaced.

Friendship. Need. Lust. Love.

He was learning her body and imagining their future together. If there had been any doubt before, there no longer was. He loved Rani Mistry, heart and soul.

He woke in the wee hours of the morning to the sound of rustling beside him. At some point, they had made it into his bed. He turned over to find Rani dressed.

"You have an early shift?" he asked softly. He didn't remember seeing an early shift for her on the schedule.

"Um. Yes." She nodded and then looked under the bed.

He sat up and leaned over the side. "What are you looking for?"

"Can't find my socks."

"Take mine." He pointed to the chest of drawers. "You know where they are, you put them there." He chuckled. "Who knew that was foreshadowing?"

He waited for Rani's quip about being such a nerdy English teacher, but instead, he was met with silence. He sat up properly. "Rani?"

"Yep?" her voice was unusually light. It was her I'm-fake-fine voice.

"Rani. What's going on?"

She shook he head. "Nothing. I should be going."

"Rani."

"Param." Her back was to him.

"Look at me."

She sighed and looked at him.

"What is going on?"

"I just think… I mean, I hope that you understand that this changes nothing." She actually looked him in the eyes as she said this crap to him.

"What do you mean changes nothing?" Param's heart thudded in his chest.

"I mean." She pressed her lips together. "We've had some sexual tension between us, since we were faking being in love. Now, it's out of our systems and we can go back to normal." She said this like she was talking about a new restaurant.

Wrong. She'd be excited about the restaurant.

"Sexual tension? Go back to normal? What are you talking about?" He hopped out of bed and grabbed his sweatpants. He needed to be standing for this. He put them on as he spoke. "I did not risk a lifetime of friendship with you for a one-night stand." He paused, his breath coming hard. "Did you?"

Rani said nothing.

"Rani. I love you and not like a friend. I am *in love* with you. I hid nothing from you last night." Param walked around to her side of the bed, and she stepped back. His stopped in his tracks as if he'd been slapped. His heart hammered in his chest as adrenaline coursed through his body.

No.

Param could not be in love with her.

Panic shook through her body, sending tears to her eyes. At least she thought the panic was making her cry. It couldn't be a broken heart.

"No. No. You can't do that. I can't love you like that."

"Rani…"

"Don't say it," she warned. If he said it again, she would cave. She would get back in that bed and give in to what her heart and body wanted and ignore that her mind warned her how horribly it could end.

She headed for the door and turned back. "I will marry you, like we decided. But I will divorce you, too."

He flinched as her words hit him like small bombs. His confusion was genuine. All the more reason she stop this before they went deeper.

"Rani…"

"Don't make this harder than it needs to be, Param," Rani said as she turned and raced down the stairs and out the door like she was ripping off a Band-Aid.

Rani wiped her eyes in the frigid cold as the door slammed behind her. She could not love him. She could not *be in* love with him. She lived her life with quick fixes, with temporary relationships. Param was her best friend, and she could not lose him.

Except that she probably just did.

She had wanted him last night, and it wasn't days or weeks of longing that she'd finally given in to. It was years. And she hadn't known it until she had known it. By then, it was too late. She had wanted to be with him, and she gave in to her feelings, not wanting to think about what the day would bring.

And then, the day brought him sleeping peacefully next to her. He was as beautiful asleep as he was awake. Her gentle giant…was not hers anymore.

It seemed she had sacrificed a lifetime of friendship for one night. Glorious night that it had been.

When she slammed the door shut behind her, she knew she'd lost her best friend.

Chapter Thirty-One

Rani actually did not have an early shift so she went home. The sun was just rising, so only her father would be awake. She entered her house, exhausted from last night's…activities, and heartbroken from the same. She entered the kitchen and found her father in there, having his morning chai, working on his crossword puzzle. It was likely two days old by now, but he would never look at the answers. But he also wouldn't leave it until it was done. The aroma of chai was so comforting, it brought tears to her eyes. Tears that she promptly swallowed.

"Hey, Papa."

"Oh, hi, beti." He looked up from his crossword. "Six-letter word for 'fooling oneself?'"

"Denial."

He wrote down the word and she found a mug and poured the rest of the chai into it. "I'll make you more if you want."

"Hm?" Her father looked at her over his half-eye glasses. "Oh. No, that's okay."

She took a sip. "Papa, this is fantastic."

He grinned at her like he had a secret.

Her jaw dropped. "You used Mom's masala!"

He put a finger to his lips. "Karina will hear you." He shrugged. "Every so often, I use it in my morning chai. Makes me feel closer to her."

She went to her father and draped an arm around his shoulders.

"What has happened?" he asked. "And are you coming home now? You didn't have an overnight."

"I was at Param's. Had a drink too many so I stayed over." It was part of the truth anyway.

"Huh." Her father studied her a moment. "Something has happened, beti. Are you in a fight with Param?"

Rani shrugged. How was she supposed to tell her father? This was a time when she missed her mother desperately.

"I am not your mother, but I love you. You can tell me anything."

"Papa, how did you know that Mom was the one?" Rani sipped her chai.

He put down his newspaper. "I didn't. We knew each other one week and we got married. We took a chance."

"That's a pretty big chance." How had she not known this?

Papa shrugged. "It worked out." He grinned.

"Did it?" Rani took another sip and looked at him.

"Well, yes. We had a lovely wedding. Your mother was a gorgeous bride. I always wondered what she saw in me. We fell in love—" he bounced his head back and forth "—slowly. We were friends almost right away.

Then our friendship led the way to a deep love. We were open and comfortable with each other." He shrugged. "We had you three girls. We practiced medicine together. We had a very good life."

"Even knowing what we know now, you would marry and fall in love with Mom again?" Rani pointed her mug at him.

He furrowed his brow. "Without hesitation. She was the love of my life. I treasure every minute we had." He looked away as if he could see those moments.

"Really?" Rani was skeptical. "Because you were a mess when she died. We all were."

He father sighed and looked at her. He was still handsome, maybe a bit of gray in his hair and beard, maybe a few pounds in his mid-section, but he worked out and ate well. He also had hazel eyes, which Sona inherited. Rani had gotten his thick hair, so she didn't care. Right now, her father's hazel eyes were focused on her.

"Beti, I know I fell apart when we lost your mother. And I know the burden of that fell to you girls. If I could change a part of my life, that is the part I would change. I would not let my grief affect you the way that it did. It is my biggest regret that I was not there for you in the way that I should have been as a parent during that time. I would give anything to have your mother back. But as long as I have you three, I still have your mom. No regrets there. So, yes. Yes, I would fall in love with your mother, knowing I would only have a short time with her." He paused, a small smile on his face. "I might treasure her a little more while I had her, however." He studied her face. "Why all the questions? Are you having trouble with Param?"

She shrugged as tears burned behind her eyes.

Her father wrapped an arm around her and pulled her into him.

She shook her head and hid her face in his sweatshirt as the sobs started. "I don't know. But I think I've lost my best friend."

"Beti, I find that hard to believe. Param loves you. Whatever it is, I'm sure if you talk it through, you will figure it out."

"I'm not sure it's that simple, Papa." She sniffed. Yes, Param loved her.

The problem was that she loved him back.

Chapter Thirty-Two

Param went to the gym. Not that he hadn't had a proper workout last night, but there was no way he was going to get any sleep, and he didn't have to be at school for another ninety minutes.

After running and lifting weights, the weight that lay heavy on his heart was still there when he entered the classroom. His students were more perceptive than he would have given them credit for.

"Hey, Mr. Sheth," Trevor said as he walked into the classroom holding Malini Sharma's hand.

"Hi, Mr. Sheth," Malini said, smiling. No turning crimson, no running away.

What? Wait until he told Rani. Nope. His heart ached. He would not be telling her.

"Hey, Trevor," Param sipped his coffee. "Hi, Malini."

"You look terrible," Malini told him.

"Thank you." Param pointed to the writing prompt. One paragraph on your favorite food and why.

"That is a lame prompt," Trevor informed him.

"It is not." Param easily slipped into seventh-grade mode.

Trevor shrugged and took a seat.

The other children came in and said hello like normal and they took their seats. They were quiet and orderly, which was in complete contrast to most days.

"Well, I have to say. You are all very quiet today. So at least I know it's possible," Param said.

"You look terrible," Josh said.

"So I've been told." Param sighed.

"The last time I looked like that, it was because Amy and I were in a fight," Malini said.

"Hmm," Param said nodding.

"What did you do to make Dr. Rani mad at you?" Josh asked.

"It's a long story." He fell in love with her.

"You should talk to Dr. Rani. Sometimes, best friends get in fights." Trevor shrugged. "Josh and I annoy each other every day."

"Every minute of every day." Josh nodded in agreement.

Param was intrigued by these children. He smiled and took a seat on the corner of his desk. "Okay. What should I say to her?"

"You should say, let's talk about why we are mad at each other," Malini said.

Param nodded. Good start. "And then what?"

"Then you have to tell the truth about why you're mad or whatever." Malini rolled her eyes. "If you aren't honest with your best friend, this won't work."

"Does this work?" Param asked, a small smile on his face.

"Usually. Everybody gets to say their feelings and then, boom! You're friends again."

"Boom, huh?" Param grinned.

"There's one problem, though," Malini added.

"What's that?"

"*You* are supposed to marry your best friend." Malini looked thoughtful. "So that is more…" She paused a moment.

"Complicated?" Param offered.

Malini pressed her lips together, a grim expression on her face. "Yes, Mr. Sheth. It's a lot more complicated."

The class nodded agreement.

"Give it a shot. The last few writing prompts have not been working for us." Josh added.

Param sighed and started the lesson. If only it were that simple.

Chapter Thirty-Three

It was a week before the wedding, so it was time for final fittings. In the interest of time, his mother was doing all the alterations. She had altered the clothes they picked and just wanted Rani and Param to try them on.

Of course, she needed them to do this together.

"Param, can you find out when Rani is free to come over for a fitting?" his mother asked. He was home for dinner. Sitting in his townhome alone had not seemed appealing today.

"Actually, Mom, can you do that? I kind of have my hands full with the play and whatnot."

The entire table fell silent. Param had never said no to reaching out to Rani.

"What?" he said as he ripped off a piece of rotli and wrapped it around some shaak.

"Why don't you want to talk to Rani?" his father asked.

"It's not that. I'm just…busy," Param insisted. His brothers weren't there, so his parents were squarely focused on him. It was a rookie move on his part.

"Text your fiancée and set up a time in the next two days. I need time to make adjustments." His mother left no room for debate.

He put the food in his mouth.

"Okay?" she pushed.

He nodded. "Okay. Fine."

He texted Rani as soon as they finished dinner. He didn't want to text her, but he wanted to argue with his mom less. Mom needs to do final fittings. LMK when you have 30 min.

The three dots showed up instantly. I get off in half an hour.

"She can be here in an hour or so, okay?" Param told his mother.

"Perfect." She nodded. "How hard was that?"

She had no idea.

"Why don't I clean up, then you can do me first so I can go home and grade papers." Param stood and started clearing the table.

"Home, he says, as if this isn't his home," his mother said.

"Mom? Seriously?"

"What are you doing?" his father asked, as if Param were committing some kind of crime.

"Cleaning up."

"You just said Rani is on her way from the hospital. Leave the food. She may be hungry. You always make sure she eats." His father eyed him suspiciously. "Have you argued?"

Param said nothing but put down the pots he had picked up. "I just have a lot of work to do."

"Very well. Leave the cleanup. Dad will do it after Rani eats. Go and put on your sherwani." His mother shooed him away. He did as she asked and went down to the family room, which was doubling as the sewing room these days.

Rani must have gotten done sooner than expected, because she showed up while his mother was assessing what more needed to be done on his outfit.

"Hey," she said as she walked into the room.

He hadn't seen or spoken to her since their night together. It was almost too much seeing her in person after having her haunt his waking and sleeping thoughts for the past couple days. She was still in scrubs, her hair in its ponytail and she was gorgeous. It was all he could do to keep from running to her and kissing her senseless. She was always beautiful as far as he was concerned. Even when she was rejecting him.

"Hey."

Her gaze traveled the length of his body as she assessed how the sherwani fit.

"Looks good, eh, beti?" his mother said from the floor where she was checking the length.

"Um. Yeah. Of course it looks good," Rani said with a small smile.

"You want to eat, beti?" his father asked.

"No. I had takeout at the hospital," Rani answered.

His parents snapped their heads to him. "She ate takeout?"

"It's fine. It was one of those company-catered things." Rani forced a giggle.

"Bland processed food. How is she supposed to treat

children if she isn't nourished properly? Is this how you treat your future wife?" His mother glared at him. But he hardly noticed because he had melted into the word "wife" while Rani had flinched at it.

"Beti, eat something after we are done here." His mother looked from her to him and back. "Go try yours on. Let's see, eh?"

Rani nodded. She glanced at him on her way up, but he looked away from her. No sooner had she hit the top of the stairs than his parents turned on him. "What happened? Why is she so distant? Why didn't you cook for her? You have been doing it for years."

"Mom. Dad. It's fine. We had...a disagreement. We're still getting married. Don't worry," Param said.

"Don't let her eat takeout." his mother reprimanded him. "You are such a fine cook. Take care of your wife. Cherish her."

"Mom." He met his mother's eyes. "Please."

She raised her hands in surrender, "Fine. I'm just saying—"

"He knows what you are saying, Veena," his father said. "Now, we leave him be, huh?"

His mother pressed her lips together to indicate she didn't like this one bit, but she wouldn't say another word.

Rani came down the stairs. She had on the cream wedding lengha, and the maroon veil pinned to the top of her head. "Wow," he said softly, and his mother squeezed his arm.

Rani was resplendent. More beautiful than he could ever put into words. His heart broke. He should get changed and go to his house to grade those papers. But he was rooted to his spot. No matter how hard it was to see her as a bride, he couldn't look away.

"Array, beti," his mother said, breathlessly. "Let me see." She walked around Rani, pulling and poking. "It's perfect." His mother put her hands on either side of Rani's face, tears in her eyes. "Your mother would be so happy." She kissed Rani's forehead, and without looking away, said, "Param. Go change. And then feed your wife-to-be."

Param came back down in his gray sweatpants and sweatshirt and started heating up food. Rani was shooed upstairs to change. She returned in her scrubs and was about to leave when Auntie called out to her.

"Sit down, beti. Param has the food ready. Uncle and I are just watching a movie in the family room."

There was no arguing with Auntie. As gentle as her tone was, she meant for Rani to eat before she left.

"Of course. That sounds great." Rani forced enthusiasm as well as a smile. She backtracked and sat down at the island where Param was making her a plate. He gently placed a plate with one fresh hot rotli and shaak in front of her.

"Make the rotli, garam-garam, Param," his mother called.

"Of course," he called.

Rani chuckled softly at the rhyme his mom made. She'd been doing it for years.

She glanced up at Param. He was not laughing. He turned back to the stove to roll out another rotli and roast it fresh for her as his mother had requested.

Rani ate the first one with the shaak. It quite literally melted in her mouth. Just as she ate the last bite, Param put a freshly buttered garam-garam rotli on her plate. "Thanks," she said.

"You're welcome," Param said, going back to the

stove. This was painful. More painful than she could have imagined.

"That's all, Param. Two is plenty."

"I've already started this one. You'll be able to finish it," he said softly.

He dropped the rotli on her plate. The aroma was incredible. He really was a great cook. He stepped back and leaned on the stove, his arms folded across his chest, and watched her eat. He had flour on his forearms and clothes, but he did not seem to care.

"Aren't you going to say anything?" she finally asked.

"There is clearly nothing to say." Param came and leaned on the island where she was sitting. "I told you how I feel. Now if you want to deny how you feel—"

"I'm not denying anything. I don't have those feelings, and you are ready to punish me for it."

"I'm not punishing you, Rani. It's called self-preservation. I can't be around you if I can't have you for real," Param whispered.

Rani stared at him, her gut filling with fear, as tears prickled her nose. "So that's it? We can't even be friends?"

Param shook his head. "No. No, Rani. We can't be friends." Her worst fears realized right in front of her. This. This was why she could not be in love with him. She wanted—no, *needed*—Param in her life.

Rani left the last rotli and stood up to leave. Then thinking twice about it, she rolled it up and ate it as she left. No sense in wasting perfectly good rotli.

There weren't going to be too many more in her future, now that the worst had happened, and she'd lost her best friend.

Chapter Thirty-Four

When Rani got home, she found her sisters opening champagne. "What's the occasion?" she asked, grabbing a glass from the bar.

"Sona broke up with Steve," Karina announced.

Rani broke into a smile. "Seriously?" She looked at Sona.

Sona grinned. "Seriously. I mean, I love him. He's a dear friend, but that's as far as it goes."

"So this is a good thing?" Rani asked.

"It's a very good thing. I can move forward with my life."

"Wait. What did Papa say?" Rani asked as Karina poured champagne.

"That was the best part. I told him that I didn't really think Steve was the right guy for me. And he said, thank god! He said he had some conversation with you the other morning, and he realized that he was putting unfair expectations on us, which is probably why Karina eloped and why I was with Steve."

"He was okay with you breaking up?" Rani couldn't believe it.

Sona nodded. "Yes. He wants me to be happy, like he was with mom. Karina too. He said you were the only one who had made proper choices based on your heart."

Rani stared at her sisters. If they only knew. But she couldn't tell them. She simply grinned and toasted her sister's newfound single-hood.

"Oh! I have those pictures for you." Sona stood.

"That's okay, I can see them later," Rani protested.

"No. You're always working. Let me grab my laptop." Sona tapped a few things into her laptop then turned it around for Rani to see.

The pictures were incredible. Sona really had some talent. Rani scrolled to the posed picture of her and Param about to kiss. Sona had captured their unexpressed feelings perfectly. Then Sona showed her the spontaneous pictures of her and Param laughing and talking. Rani hadn't realized that Sona had been taking pictures the whole time.

"Oh my god!" Karina said from beside her. "Look at how he's looking at you here."

It was one of the pictures that Sona had been trying to pose but the two of them kept laughing. Param's attention was squarely on her, and her head was slightly turned as she looked back at him. There was flat-out naked love on his face as he focused on her and her only. There was nothing else in the world for him at that moment.

Her own face revealed her feelings as well. Anyone

could see that the woman in the picture was in love with the man she was looking at.

Tears blossomed in her eyes. What was happening?

"Look how much he loves you. And he's not even afraid to show it." Karina squeezed her shoulders. "You two are the cutest. And you both waited long enough to discover it." She chuckled.

The pictures blurred in her tears. She wiped them away. "Sona. Finish college, but you have talent as a photographer."

"Absolutely!" Karina agreed. "I'd be happy to help you with a website."

Sona flushed and shrugged her shoulders. "You think?"

"You made Rani cry, the pictures were so beautiful. And she is a rock." Karina laughed.

Rani shoved her sister a little. "Am not."

"Are so," Sona agreed.

"Don't you remember? We used to tease you for not having any friends, except Param? You would say you would never give your heart to anyone, because a broken heart would never heal," Karina remembered.

"Well, I wasn't wrong," Rani defended herself.

"Yes. Well. At least you gave your heart to Param." Karina motioned to the computer.

Rani was done with this conversation. "I'm going to bed. Early shift tomorrow. Hey, Sona, can I borrow one your long gowns?"

"Sure. For what?"

"I'm going to a fundraiser gala thing next week."

"Well, let's pick out a dress so Param can coordinate." Sona was halfway up the stairs.

"I'm not going with Param," she blurted out.

"Who are you going with?"

"Well, it's a fundraiser, but I'm going to pitch to people about the free clinic," Rani explained.

Karina narrowed her eyes. "Who are you going with, Rani?"

"Oh, uh, Deep Kulkarni."

"You're going to a fundraiser with your ex?" Sona almost yelled. "Does Param know about this?"

"Sure. I told him about it." And then they argued and had mind-blowing sex.

Param kept himself busy with play practice and school over the next few days. He dropped off food to the ED when he knew Rani was on shift. It was easier than another lecture from his parents. They kept calling and texting to be sure he was feeding her. It was getting tiring. He left the food for her at the nurses' station and they promised to get it to her. Luckily, the wedding was only a few days off.

Though he wasn't sure how he was going to live in the same house with Rani after they got married. He was grading papers in his office when he heard his front door open, followed by his brothers' voices. He closed his eyes and inhaled. He just wanted to be alone. But he heard them traipsing up the stairs, chatting and laughing.

They bounded into his office much like the way they used to bound into his room when they were kids—loud and uninvited.

"I'm busy." He grumped at them.

"We have something for you that will cheer you up," Milan said

"I don't need cheering up." He didn't raise his head from his desk.

"Not according to mom and dad," Nishant said, his voice serious where Milan's voice had been light.

Param looked up at Nishant and made pointed eye contact. "Everything is fine. Not to worry."

Nishant nodded understanding.

"The parents said you had some kind of argument with Rani, which I am sure is your fault. But we have something that will fix all that." Milan was nearly busting with excitement.

Param turned to his younger brother. "Yeah? What's that?"

Milan pulled a ring box from his pocket. "Done early."

Param stared at the box as if it were lethal.

"Well, come on. Open it. Then we need to make sure you propose properly." Milan took off his coat and rested it on a chair. "Honestly, you'd think you were better with women."

Param looked at his brothers and then back at the box. His stomach was in knots, his heart heavy with dread. He reached for the box, his hands shaking slightly. This did not go unnoticed.

"Bhai." Milan's voice filled instantly with compassion. "Whatever the fight was, it'll be fine. It's Rani after all."

Param picked up the box.

Rani would never wear these rings. Not really. Every interaction with her was painful. He'd lost a confidante, a support system, a friend and the woman he loved all in one fail swoop.

"Listen, Aisha and I fought a few days before our wedding—it's stress. It'll be fine," Milan assured him.

Param chuckled. His little brother was taking care of him. "You're right. We're still getting married." Param opened the box and smiled. The rings were beautiful; Rani was going to love them. He'd have to find a way for her to keep them, even though they wouldn't be together.

"They're perfect," he told his brothers.

"Hey, how come Rani doesn't have a lot of stuff here?" Milan asked.

"She's been busy. She brings stuff with her each time she comes over."

"Well, there's a snowstorm coming in a few days. We can help move the rest of her stuff before that."

Param's heart was heavy, but he forced himself to smile at his brother in gratitude.

"I'll let her know."

Chapter Thirty-Five

Rani slipped on the black fitted gown she had borrowed from Sona. Nothing too fancy, just a simple, black, one-shoulder gown that hugged her curves (she was a bit fuller than Sona). She put on some dangling sparkly earrings, put her hair in a messy bun and then last minute borrowed heels from Sona as well.

Deep had texted earlier that he would send a car, even though Rani insisted she could certainly drive herself. But at the allotted time, the driver messaged her that he was waiting outside the house.

"Wow, beti. You look amazing," her father said.

"Thanks, Papa."

"Tell Param I said hello," he said, involved in his crossword again.

"I'm not going with Param." She dropped a lipstick and her phone into her clutch.

Her father left the crossword and looked at her. "What?"

"I'm going to a fundraising gala to pitch about the free clinic. I'm told there may be people there who would be interested in making significant donations."

"Oh. Well then, good luck. Be careful on the road. It's snowing."

"Oh, Deep sent a car. So don't worry," Rani told her father.

"Deep?"

"Yes. His father throws this gala."

He furrowed his brow. "Deep Kulkarni? The neuro guy?"

"That's him."

"Be safe, beti. Enjoy."

Rani grabbed Sona's dress coat (why not?) and went out to the car. The snow was definitely coming down hard. The sidewalks and streets were already thick with snow. She was quite grateful that Deep had sent the car. Now she wouldn't have to worry about parking and walking in these shoes.

Twenty minutes later, the car dropped her off in front of Deep's dad's building. The driver handed her a card with his number for when she was ready to go home. A bellman opened her door, and she thanked the driver before exiting the car. There was an awning to shield her from the snow, which had gotten even thicker in the past twenty minutes. Another bellman opened the door for her and she easily located the elevator.

Rani took the elevator up to the penthouse as instructed by Deep. She stepped off the elevator into a gorgeous penthouse with people milling about. The sound of a DJ playing music reached her from another room. People were chattering and laughing and clinking glasses.

She walked in and a waiter offered her a glass of champagne. She took it because she needed something to calm her nerves. She had practiced her pitch many times to Cami, who said it was fabulous and that anyone who turned her down must have a heart of stone.

The penthouse had many rooms, and the music was coming from the largest one in the back. Rani preferred to stay where she was, hearing people but not being in the middle of them.

Deep had mentioned dancing was part of the night. She might be interested after she was done pitching. But the reality was that the past few days had drained her. She missed Param. He was a huge part of her life, and now that part was an empty gaping hole. Well, in a few months, she would have to find something to fill that gap. If she was lucky tonight, she'd be getting a pediatric free clinic off the ground.

She was admiring the décor when a warm and familiar voice called her name. "Rani!"

She turned to find Deep walking towards her, accompanied by a very attractive woman in a lovely but clearly expensive evening gown that perfectly matched the deep blue in Deep's bow tie.

"Deep." Rani beamed at him, nodding at the woman. She did look lovely on Deep's arm. Maybe Param was partially right about Deep. "Thanks so much for the opportunity. What a lovely place."

"Of course. I'm so glad you made it. I'd like you to meet my fiancée, Tracy." He indicated the woman beside him. "Tracy is an attorney in private practice, but she can also be a valuable resource to you as you move forward with the clinic."

"What? You're engaged? You kept that secret." She extended her hand to Tracy. "Rani Mistry, so nice to meet you. Congratulations! And yes, it's always fabulous to have a lawyer on your side." Rani found she was very happy for Deep. Not one ounce of regret or jealousy. Just happy that someone she cared about was happy.

"Well," Tracy shook her hand, "I have heard so much about you."

Rani widened her eyes.

"All good," Tracy laughed. "And all in the past. I am so excited about your clinic. Please reach out—I'd love to help in any way that I can." Tracy was warm and genuine. Rani liked her immediately.

"Rani is getting married as well, Tracy," Deep said.

"You heard?" Rani asked.

"Of course. Congrats to you as well."

"Thank you." Sadness filled her. She forced the smile to stay on her face and excitement into her voice. "Next week in fact!"

"That's fabulous," Tracy said. "Listen, I know you're here to work, but Deep's parents hired a fabulous DJ and the food is to die for. Please eat and enjoy." She squeezed Rani's hand. "So great meeting you. I'll let Deep introduce you around. I have some colleagues to catch up with."

"I will find you later," Rani said.

Tracy nodded and gave her fiancé a quick kiss before leaving.

Rani watched her go and then turned to Deep. "You are glowing, I'm so happy for you."

"She's amazing," Deep said as he watched Tracy

mingle. "Let me show you around this place. It's my parents' penthouse. I'll make the intros as we walk."

He led her around the penthouse pointing out the various views from the floor-to-ceiling windows.

"Wow, what a gorgeous view of the harbor." She sighed. The water was almost black in the moonlight. The snow seemed to have stopped as suddenly as it came, but there was an easy six to eight inches on the ground. Param would love this view. She shook her head at the thought. It did not matter what Param would love.

"This place is incredible." Rani looked all around, trying to take it all in. Natural wood floors, sparse décor, the place was beautiful, but it hardly looked like people lived there. The guests were beautiful as well. She saw designer after designer dresses and suits. She only knew about these things because Sona was obsessed with fashion and knew all the designers. Rani wanted to take pictures to show Sona where her clothes had hung out.

"Ah, here we go," he said as they approached an older couple. "Drs. Eric and Sejal Gor. This is Dr. Rani Mistry."

Rani shook hands and started her pitch. No sooner had they shown interest than Deep introduced to her another potential donor. And so the evening went for the next couple of hours.

They had walked past the room with the DJ and the music was very loud. It was very good but she couldn't really hear the DJ. They kept walking and meeting people. She gave her pitch to those who seemed interested.

Some of the people were not interested, but a few were impressed with what she was proposing, and shared their emails with her so they could be in touch.

A couple hours and a couple glasses in, Rani was feeling pretty good about the clinic.

"Thanks again, Deep. I'd love to see Tracy and check out that DJ," Rani said. She was loathe to go home and be alone with her thoughts.

"Of course." Deep started to walk with her but got pulled away. "You go on ahead."

Rani was more than happy to do so now that the work part of the evening was over. She ran into Tracy who was dancing with some friends and they invited her to join them.

Rani enjoyed the music and dancing, but her thoughts continued to drift to Param. She was about to call it a night after a couple songs when Deep found her, his face lit with excitement.

"Rani! You're not going to believe this!" Deep shouted because they had drifted close to the DJ. He glanced at Tracy and her eyes lit up.

"Tell her!"

"Tell me what?" Rani asked.

"You got it!"

Her heart pounded. Surely he wasn't saying what she thought he was saying? She couldn't have…not so fast.

But Deep was nodding his head, the most ridiculous grin on his face, and Tracy was nearly jumping up and down.

"You got funding," Deep said. "A large donation and a grant."

Rani could hardly believe her ears and tears prickled at her nose and her vision went blurry. It was everything she could have ever hoped for—sure there were details, but still—she was going to have the free clinic.

As her tears of relief fell, the only person she wanted to talk to was the one man she couldn't talk to anymore.

"That is fantastic!" She spontaneously flung her arms around Deep and hugged him, giving him a quick peck on the cheek, she was so happy. "I couldn't have done it without you!" She pulled back and he handed her a handkerchief. She took it and hugged him again, pulling him tight in her gratitude and excitement. "Thank you! Thank you so much!"

Someone tapped her shoulder, and she turned around. Milan. The DJ was DJ eM. She saw Aisha coming up behind Milan. DJ Ai.

"What the hell are you doing?" Milan's eyes were hard and angry.

Aisha came up behind him. "Milan, relax, I don't want you getting all worked up."

"I'm fine, Aisha. I just want to know what Rani is doing hugging—" he glared at Deep "—her ex-boyfriend, who happens to be my doctor?"

Aisha looked from Deep to Rani, clearly confused.

"Oh Milan." Rani started. "It's not like that. See Deep was just helping me out—in fact, meet Tracy, his—"

Just then, Rani's phone, Milan's phone and Aisha's phone all dinged at the same time. The three of them looked at one another then hastily pulled out their phones.

Nishant had texted them all.

It was Param.

Chapter Thirty-Six

Param and Angelina walked into the vestibule of the school building after a late-running play practice. The snow was coming down so hard that it was difficult to see anything but white.

"Um, Angelina, I'm going to guess that living in Texas you didn't get much practice driving in this kind of weather?" Param asked.

Angelina eyed the snow with trepidation. "You would guess correctly."

"Would you like a ride home? We can go around the corner and grab a pizza and see if it dies down some and then I'll drop you off," Param offered.

"That sounds fabulous. Your fiancée won't mind?" she asked.

"Nope." Not one damn bit.

They got into his car and he drove them to the pizza

place. They ordered and sat down with their sodas and pizza.

"I want to apologize about not necessarily being up-front about Rani when we first met. I know I gave you the wrong impression, but Rani and I are…complicated," Param offered as they ate. "It was wrong of me, and I apologize."

"Thank you for saying that. I understand complicated. But you saying so makes it easier to work together," Angelina said. "Pizza is on me tonight. It's the least I can do for the ride home."

"If you don't mind me asking," Angelina said as they ate their pizza, "what exactly is the deal with you and Rani?"

"We're getting married," Param answered. He took a bite of his pizza, hardly even tasting it.

"You said it was complicated."

"Very."

"You are both clearly fond of each other, you have a long history—"

"She's not in love with me," Param blurted out. It was as if he'd been waiting to say the words out loud, to tell someone the whole truth.

"Well, *that's* not true." Angelina was quite matter-of-fact about that.

"She's marrying me so that we can unlock this trust my grandfather had set up for me and my brothers. We need the money because my youngest brother needs to have a tumor removed from his brain in an experimental procedure overseas. We're pretending to be in love so we can convince the keeper of the trust that we really are getting married." Param paused for breath. *OMG*. Did he just tell a near stranger their whole plan? He closed his eyes and put his slice down. "I'm sorry. I never should have—"

Angelina frowned and shook her head. "No, that makes sense. I love my siblings fiercely, as well. I would marry someone if it helped them." She eyed him. "But that doesn't change my statement. Rani *is* in love with you. No matter what she says." She sipped her soda. "Which is why I didn't like her when I first met her."

Param opened his mouth to apologize again.

"Do not apologize again. I'm a grown woman and once I saw what was between you two, I knew I had to move on." She rolled her eyes. "It's obvious to everyone how you both feel about each other."

"Except to her," Param said sadly.

Angelina grinned and picked up another slice. "Isn't that always the case? We are always the last ones to know what is good for us."

He knew what was good for him. Rani Mistry was good for him. The question was whether or not he was good for her.

For that, he had no answer.

Angelina kept up a running dialogue about the play, and he was grateful to have that to focus on. He hardly remembered that he was getting married later this week. Or maybe he was better off not thinking about it. He and Rani would be married very soon whether they wanted to be or not. The trust would open and then after an agonizing month of pretending to be newlyweds, Rani would divorce him. Talking to Angelina about the play was simply a distraction.

The snow had died down some, and the temperature had dropped, so the roads were quite slick by the time they finished eating and headed out. Angelina had held on to his arm to navigate the black ice in the parking lot.

"I promise I am not hitting on you." She had tried to laugh while her eyes had shown slight terror as she slipped and slid her way to the car. "I've never had to do this before."

Param had chuckled and given her pointers on what kind of shoes to invest in for Northeastern winters.

He seated her safely in the passenger seat and made his way to driver's side, but not without a slippery incident himself. *The roads must be awful.*

Param carefully pulled out of the small lot, hoping the roads had at least been salted. But not only had the roads not been salted, the plows had not been out yet. Angelina tracked the plows on an app and told him the major highways like 95 were plowed, but the smaller roads had not yet been touched.

"Well, we have plenty of gas, so I'll drive slow," Param said. He was driving slowly and carefully, clearing the few back streets safely, and moving on to a small highway that had not been plowed but had some traffic. It was difficult to make out the lanes, but Param tried to follow the tracks laid out by earlier cars.

He was navigating fairly well and so slowed down a bit to take the exit for Angelina's place. He glanced in his side mirrors and rearview to clear the lanes, when he was blinded by headlights from the rearview that approached with increasing speed.

He flung his arm out in front of Angelina as the sound of metal crunching metal reached him along with her scream. His head hit the windshield, even with the buffer of the airbag. The car slid on ice and spun out, finally stopped when it hit a guardrail. The driver's side door was crushed into him, and pain radiated in his arm and head. As his consciousness faded, he had the thought that he hoped Rani didn't see him this way.

And then, everything went black.

Chapter Thirty-Seven

Rani hopped into the back of Milan and Aisha's van, with Deep just behind her. The roads were slick so Aisha drove carefully. Param was at Howard County Hospital, which was near home, but not near here. The twenty-five-minute ride to the hospital was excruciating.

"Just pull up to the doors. I'll get out there," Rani said to Aisha. If Rani could have transported herself to the hospital, it wouldn't have been fast enough. She flashed back to being forced to stay at home with Veena Auntie when her mother was in the hospital. She couldn't do that again.

Everything she had eaten was threatening to come up.

She needed to focus so she could tend to Param. But she needed to get to him first and everything around her had slowed down, as if the universe did not understand that the man she loved could be dying and she needed to save him.

Aisha glanced at Rani in the rearview mirror and nodded. "Sure thing." No sooner had Aisha slowed down the car than Rani was sliding back the door and jumping out of the car, still in the tight dress and heels. She tripped and landed on all fours, scraping her hands and tearing the dress, but she was up in an instant, completely unaware of anyone around her.

She just needed to get to Param. Her stomach was in knots, her hands were shaking and tears threatened to pour down her face. She refused to let any of that matter. She became aware of the fact that her sisters were in the waiting room with her father. She saw Param's parents with them. They all stood as she passed. She put up a hand to stop them. She needed to get information before she could share it. She walked up to the nurses' station.

"Where is he?" she asked as softly and calmly as she could.

"Dr. Mistry." Marc moved back from the desk and tilted his head for Rani to follow. Rani followed the nurse to a glass-walled room with the curtains drawn.

"He's in here. His brother is with him."

The chart was in the small box outside the room. Rani grabbed it.

"Dr. Mistry, you're not supposed—"

Rani raised one eyebrow and dared the nurse to continue.

"Never mind."

Rani quickly scanned his chart to prepare her for whatever was on the other side. He had a broken arm. Well, he'd had two of them in the time she'd known him. He'd come in the ambulance unconscious. Rani steeled herself and walked through the door.

Rani was a trained ED physician. She saw children banged up in car accidents, fallen from trees, injured in playground accidents and from fights. She'd seen them sicker than they'd ever been. But she always kept calm, kept herself together because that was her job. Stay calm and help the children.

She drew on her training as she opened the door and pushed aside the curtain. It failed her almost immediately.

Param. *Her Param* was lying in that bed, with his arm in a sling and his head in a bandage that had blood seeping from it. His eyes were closed and he was paler than she'd ever seen him.

The machines beeped and slurped, dinged and zinged. All sounds of a healthy body being monitored. Tears of relief spilled from her eyes, and she didn't even try to hold herself back from leaping to his side.

"Param."

Nothing.

"Param," she said his name louder.

"He's been out since we got here," Nishant said from the corner.

"How long?"

Nishant shook his head. "I don't know. Maybe an hour. Angelina is next door."

"What?"

"She was in the car with him."

"He needs an MRI." Jealousy strong and hard welled up inside her.

"He had a CT, and it was clean. We're waiting to see if he can get an MRI."

Rani looked at Param. "Wait here, Nishant."

She ran out to the waiting room as fast as the heels

would let her. "Deep." She looked around. "Where's Deep? I need him here."

Deep and Tracy had left the event along with them, at Rani's request, when Nishant's text indicated that Param was unconscious.

"I bet you do," said Milan from the corner.

Rani ignored him.

"He's getting coffee," offered Karina, sending a what-the-hell look to Milan.

Deep and Tracy came up behind her, holding many coffee cups.

"Deep. Do something. He's unconscious." Rani fought for her doctor voice, but she was begging. "He's been out for like an hour. He could have a bleed or something."

"Rani." Deep's voice was slow and calm. "We cannot do an MRI on an unconscious person."

"Deep, please." Tears came to her eyes again. She swallowed her sob as she took his arm and begged Deep to perform a miracle for her.

"All I can do is admit him and watch him."

Rani nodded vigorously. "Yes. Do that." She squeezed his arm.

"I can't believe you," Milan said to her, shaking his head. He looked at the room. "I saw her hugging him tonight. And she's supposed to marry Param in a few days…" Milan shook his head. "I have known you most of my life and you have never been the cheating…" Milan slowed his speech and looked around the room. Everyone was there. Her sisters, Pankthi, her father, Param's parents and Patel Dada. Milan landed his gaze on Rani. "Wait."

"Hey." Angelina popped her head in the waiting room. "How is he?"

"You were in the car with him?" Rani fought to keep her voice neutral. This poor woman was also in the car.

"Yes." She nodded.

"How are you?"

Angelina looked at the family and back to Rani. "I'm okay. Just some scratches and bruises."

"What happened?"

"We had gone to dinner—we were just grabbing a pizza after play practice."

He had taken her to dinner. It was two colleagues simply getting a bite together after work. But Rani wanted to interrogate her.

What did he say?

How did he seem?

Did he smile?

Did he laugh?

Was he angry with me?

"The roads were slick. He offered to drive me home because I have no experience on these kinds of roads," Angelina continued.

Rani nodded. Of course he did.

"We were doing fine, it seemed. Until someone hit his car from the back. The airbags kicked in, but I remember his arm flying out and pushing me back." She paused her gaze on Milan. "It's probably how he broke it."

It was his right arm that was broken.

"I'm not injured because of him." She looked Rani in the eye. "You're a very lucky woman. He's not just a pretty face with muscles, you know? He's the real deal."

Rani nodded, holding back her tears.

"And you." She squeezed Milan's hand. "You are the luckiest brother. Param told me all about the fake wedding to get to your grandfather's trust. It's incredible. There is nothing like that sibling bond."

Rani's mouth gaped open. Milan stared at Angelina.

Angelina sighed. "Well, my sister is coming up from DC to get me. Please keep me posted? I know the students will be worried, and I'd like to let them know he'll be…" She hesitated.

"Yes, of course." Rani turned her back on the room while Angelina left. She and Param had just been outed, and Patel Dada was in the room.

"Rani." Milan spoke to her.

She turned to face him.

"What the hell was she talking about?" Milan demanded.

"She said, dear husband." Aisha came up beside him. "That your crazy family loves you so much, that your brother and his best friend were pretending to be in love to get married to help you."

Milan looked at his wife and then around the waiting room, and Rani followed his gaze. But there was only one other surprised face in the room: Patel Dada.

"None of you look surprised," Rani said.

"Did you all know?" Milan asked

"Yes, kid. We know," said Karina.

"Yep," agreed Sona.

"We were hoping that if they went through the process, they would realize how they felt about each other, and it would be real by the time they got married," Auntie said.

"They just needed that little nudge," Papa added. Her father knew?

Rani ran her gaze around this room of people who loved Param, and loved her, and her heart filled.

"We all knew, Rani. Just not Milan," Pankthi offered.
Milan turned to his wife. "You knew?"

"Like I was going to stop anything that might help
you," Aisha said fiercely.

Whatever was going on here, it could wait. Rani
needed to make sure Param was okay.

She practically ran to Param's room. She hadn't seen
Param since they had their final fittings for their wedding outfits. What was the last thing she'd said to him?

She could not take her eyes off him. She pulled up
the chair in the room and slid it over closer to the bed,
so she could touch him. She took his hand in both of
hers and kissed it, before holding it against her heart.
Her heart was breaking. What if he didn't wake up?
Which was ridiculous, because he had to. He had to.

*Her mother had looked weak and pale like this. But
had spoken to Rani. Why wasn't Param awake?*

"This is why, Param," she said through tears. "This
is why I can't be with you. I can't do this. I can't lose
you. My dad never recovered from losing my mother.
He still does not even sleep in their room."

"You're not going to lose me," he groaned.

Rani looked up at him. "You're awake." All new tears
flooded down her cheeks. "You're awake."

He looked up at her smiled. "Yeah, I'm awake." He
wiggled his fingers. "And I like where my hand is." He
drew his gaze over her. "You look hot. Did you dress
up just to sit next to me in the hospital so I'd wake up.
Because if I had known you'd be wearing that, I would
have woken up sooner." He gave her a lazy, sleepy grin
that she'd only just seen for the first time a week ago.

"Oh my god!" She put her hands on the sides of his
head and kissed him.

"Oh. Kisses too? I should hit my head more often." His voice was groggy, but he managed a very sexy smile. Or maybe he was just tired?

"Dccp! Deep!" Rani called out.

He winced. "The shouting is not good. Definitely not shouting other men's names. I feel like I could make you scream mine, though." He tried to sit and scrunched up his face in pain and lay back down. "Maybe later. When the pounding in my head stops."

Chapter Thirty-Eight

Param tried to open his eyes as Rani ran to the door. She looked delicious in that dress, and he didn't want to miss a second of her in it.

"I need neuro in here. He's awake." Her voice was higher pitched and faster than normal. Like she was... scared.

Crap. He was scaring her.

Nishant entered with Deep close behind him. Deep was in a tuxedo. Param looked at Rani then Deep. They had been out together. It was coming back to him. The reason they had argued. Fundraiser. Pitching for the clinic.

"Well, Param." Deep approached. "Good to see you awake."

"Is it?" Param squinted at him.

Deep managed a chuckle (fake as far as Param was concerned). He did a check, which involved Param following his finger, looking at a light and a bunch of other things that seemed ridiculous, but Rani was watching closely.

And he was watching her.

She nodded every time Deep moved to another test. When he finished, he wrote a few things in the chart and turned to Param. "You probably have a concussion, so we're going to admit you for observation, hopefully just overnight."

Param nodded, but his head throbbed every time he did that. "Yeah. Okay." He snuck another glance at Rani. Deep followed his gaze.

"Yes. Well, someone will be by as soon as we get a room upstairs."

"Thanks," Param said, automatically, his attention still on Rani. Rani, meanwhile, was following Deep out of the room.

"Hey, little brother. Tired of Milan getting all the attention?" Nishant came over and stood in front of him.

"What are they talking about out there?" Param asked.

Nishant looked toward the door. "Hmm. Two doctors standing in a hallway chatting. Probably talking about having sex together tonight."

"What?" Param snapped his head to Nishant and all kinds of small and large hammers pounded the inside and outside of his brain.

Nishant chuckled then shook his head. "It's too easy. They're talking about you, the patient."

"They're standing really close."

"They're talking softly so the whole hospital can't hear them," Nishant said. "And we met his fiancée."

"His what?"

"You heard me. He's engaged."

Param eyed Nishant, then slowly lay back on the bed. He was feeling woozy, but he didn't think it was all because of his accident.

"You okay?" Nishant asked. "Just so you know, she's a rock when she works, but she lost it seeing you here."

"She looks hot in that dress," he said with his eyes closed. "But she always looks hot."

"Hey!" His mother's voice reached him from the door. He raised a hand in greeting. "Mom."

He opened his eyes and grinned as first his parents, then Rani's dad, then Pankthi, then Sona and Karina and finally, Milan and Aisha came to see that he was alive and well. Rani re-entered the room, standing back while the family checked on him.

An orderly with a wheelchair arrived to take him to his room and the family cleared out, saying they were going home and would return in the morning.

Rani walked up to the floor with him, in her bare feet, the gown dragging on the ground. Her eye makeup was smeared, her hair cascaded down her back in messy waves.

She said nothing.

The orderly wheeled him into his room, then helped him to bed. Rani stared out the window.

"Okay. I'm Melissa, your night nurse. I'm sure your family will be bringing you a few things, but in the meantime, I can get you each a set of scrubs so you'll be more comfortable." The nurse was a middle-aged woman who took charge of a situation. "Though," she said, smiling at Param, "the way you're looking at her, you clearly like the dress on her."

"She's beautiful in scrubs, too," he said softly and caught a smirk on Rani's face.

Melissa chuckled. "I bet she is."

The nurse left and returned with two sets of scrubs. "Here you go. Ring the bell if you need anything else."

"Thank you," Rani said. She took one set of scrubs and went to the bathroom to change. Param tried to stand to change, but the room started to spin and he collapsed back onto the bed.

Rani emerged from the bathroom, her hair in a ponytail—*did women just keep hair ties all over the place?*—and dressed in scrubs.

She came around to where he was sitting. "Here, let me help you. You're probably super dizzy."

"You trying to get me to take my clothes off?" Param grinned.

Rani rolled her eyes. "Lift your arm out."

He did as he was told. She gripped the end of one sleeve. The other was already in a sling under the sweater. "Pull your arm in." He did so, watching her face the whole time. She avoided his gaze. Once his arm was out, she bunched up the bottom of his sweater and pulled it gently over his head.

He winced as the movement made his head hurt.

"Sorry." She moved the sweater more slowly over his head. Then she bunched up the scrub top and placed it gently over his head.

"I'll need you to stand," she said softly, still not looking him in the eye.

He sighed and took her offered hand to balance as he stood. He undid the zipper of his jeans and tried to pull them down, but his world spun again and he collapsed once more to the bed.

"Param, just let me do this. I'm a doctor."

He looked up at her. "Right." She was a professional.

She did this all the time. There was nothing intimate about letting her dress him. Not for her.

Just for him.

She helped him out of his pants and into the scrub bottoms, which involved a whole lot of leaning on her, so he didn't fall over. The whole time she undressed and dressed him, not one comment about how overly big his muscles were, or how ridiculously tall he was. None of the things they used to laugh about.

When he was dressed, she tucked him into bed. He waited for her to leave, but instead, she moved the one big chair in the room closer to the bed, grabbed a blanket and curled up in it.

"I thought the family was coming."

"Nope. It's midnight. They went home. The roads—" Her voice caught and he shifted his eyes to look at her. She swallowed hard. "The roads are bad."

"You're telling me."

"This is not a joke, Param Sheth," she snapped at him, her words watery with tears and anger. "Everything out of your mouth since this happened has been a joke."

"Side effect of the concussion."

"GRRR."

"Did you just growl at me?"

She glared at him.

"Not everything has been a joke," he said quietly.

"Really?" she snapped.

"I wasn't joking about you being beautiful in scrubs."

She looked away from him.

Chapter Thirty-Nine

She was going to have to tell him. She was going to have to tell him before someone in the family did.

They lost the money for Milan. All that prep for a wedding, all the clothes, and the planning and the pictures and the engagement party—for nothing. All because she went and hugged Deep Kulkarni—which was completely innocent—and the fact that Milan's brain worked just fine even with that damn tumor in it. Not to mention that Angelina had spilled his beans as well.

She had no idea what to make of the fact that the families had known about their ruse all along and went along with it because they thought Rani and Param should be together. She might be able to excuse the Sheth family, but her sisters? Her father? They should know better. They should know her better.

She would never make a commitment like that. It

was too scary. If the incidents of tonight did not prove that, she did not know what did.

When she thought the worst had happened to Param, she had lost all sense of anything but him. She looked at her feet. She didn't even know where her shoes were.

"Where are your shoes?" Param asked from the bed. The lights were off, but Rani had not yet pulled the nightshade down, so a trickle of moonlight mixed with streetlights lit the room.

She sighed. "I must have taken them off somewhere. It's all very blurry. I have a pair of clogs in my locker in ED, I just never got them." She looked at him. Tousled hair, more scruff than usual, amused eyes despite the paleness of his features.

"How's Angelina?" he asked suddenly as if he'd only just realized that she had been in the car.

"She's fine. Good. Her sister came from DC to be with her, but she only has a few scratches." Rani paused, smiling proudly at him. "Thanks to you."

He furrowed his brow at her. She nodded at his broken arm. "You reached out to push her back when your car was first hit. That's how you broke it."

"Really?"

"Yes. You may now add hero to your résumé." Though he had always kind of been hers anyway.

He nodded and closed his eyes. Rani let him sleep for a bit. She fell asleep in the chair and was awakened about an hour later when the nurses came to take vitals and check his machines.

He was good, so they turned out the light and left. "I thought I wasn't allowed to sleep if I had a concussion."

"Old protocol. Right now they want to be sure you aren't getting worse."

"The headache seems less." He turned in the bed to face her. "What happened today?"

"You had a car accident."

"Before that."

She should just tell him now. The family would be here with chai and snacks in a matter of hours.

"I went to that fundraiser with Deep," she said softly.

"That much I could tell. You looked amazing," he said. "He looked like a doctor in a tux. Boring."

She rolled her eyes. "It was a legit fundraiser, and I did pitch to people about the free clinic and …" She grinned as she remembered. "I got a grant and a large donation."

"What?" Param tried to sit up, but winced and lay back down. "That's fabulous! I'm so proud of you."

She nodded. "You were wrong about him."

He looked abashed. "I heard about his fiancée." He shrugged. "I was jealous."

"You should know she is a lovely person. And she also looks good on his arm," Rani chuckled.

"So I was a tiny bit right. And a whole lot of jerk." He smiled at her.

"So, you told Angelina about our little plan?" Rani raised an eyebrow.

"I did." He paused. "Wait. How do you know?"

"She told the whole waiting room when Milan tried to accuse me of cheating on you."

"You cheated on me?"

"I hugged Deep. When he told me about the donation. His fiancée was standing right there." Rani waved him off. "Milan was looking out for you."

"So, Milan was suspicious, and then Angelina inadvertently confirmed to everyone who was sitting in the waiting room, which included Patel Dada."

Param sighed. "So, no money."

Rani shook her head. "No." She paused. "And it turns out that the whole family knew about us faking the whole time. They went along with it because they thought we should be together and they agreed that the trust money was needed for Milan."

Param could not process what Rani was saying. And it wasn't the concussion. He did not want to process what Rani saying. That they would not be getting the money from the trust.

"It's just as well."

"What do you mean?"

"I mean—" Her voice broke. "It's just as well that the family knows we were faking. We're not going to be together anyway."

"Rani. What are you saying? Are you saying that you don't love me?"

His heart nearly stopped beating while he waited for her answer. If Rani did not love him, then no one would. And he didn't even care. The only one he wanted was Rani.

"No," she nearly spat at him, her eyes watery with tears. "That is not what I'm saying. I'm saying that I do love you, but I cannot—will not—be with you."

"But, Rani—"

"You. Were. In. A. Car. Accident. *You*." She shook her head at him. "I cannot keep watching people I love die—"

"I did not die," Param said softly.

"But you could have." She shot back at him. Tears streamed down her face in earnest now, she wasn't even trying to stop them.

"I can't have you in my life and not be with you. I

cannot promise that nothing will happen to me. But I can't be just friends with you, either."

She nodded and wiped away her tears.

"I am not your mother."

"I know. My mother is gone." Rani stood and looked away from him.

He was awakened by the nurse coming to check his vitals for the umpteenth time, but this time, the sun was up and Rani's chair was empty. The sight made him sadder than he might have thought possible.

He had been wrong last night.

He didn't care how he had Rani, he just wanted her in his life. No matter how painful, he'd rather see her and talk to her just like he had for the past twenty years than to have that void in his life.

He would rather have her as a friend, with all the pain and angst that would come with that, than not have her at all.

"Ah, there he is." His parents were at the door. Followed by Milan and Aisha. His mother came in and walked right to his bed. "How are you, beta? Did you sleep?"

His father walked in behind her carrying not one, but two brown shopping bags that he knew were filled with food. And most definitely, at least one thermos of chai.

"You didn't need all those snacks. I'm probably going home today." Param shook his head. Wow. Almost no hammers.

"You never know," his mother said. "Pinku Auntie went to the hospital to have something checked overnight, so we didn't send any snacks or food. Then she ended up staying for a week."

"She had a heart attack, Mom," Param reminded her.

"All I am saying is, you never know." She reached into one bag and produced what he had been waiting for. The thermos of chai. She poured him some in a paper cup.

Param sipped the chai. It was seriously the best damn chai he'd ever had. "Mom, this chai is incredible."

She beamed. "Sachin Uncle. He used—"

"Auntie's special masala? But why? He's had that saved in his freezer for years."

"I don't know. He showed up this morning and said to bring this to you and Rani." She looked around. "Where is she?"

"I don't know. She stayed all night, but she was gone when I woke up."

"Hey, Bhai." Milan came over to hug him.

"Hey, little brother. Sorry that our plan didn't work. But I already have ideas for getting the money—"

"Whoa. Stop. I just came to see my big brother and make sure he's okay. That's all. No talk of tumors or fake weddings or anything," Milan said. "I can't believe you would go through all of that for me."

"It was Rani's idea."

"Well, duh. Of course it was. She's the schemer between the two of you." Milan smiled as he shook his head.

Aisha came over and hugged Param. "You okay, Bhai?"

"I've been better, but I feel better than yesterday."

Aisha squeezed his hands. "Glad to hear it." She looked around. "Where's Rani?"

"I was just telling Mom that I have no idea where she is. She was here all night. She was gone when I woke up."

"Hello." They all turned to see Patel Dada in the doorway. "I came to see how Param is doing."

Param sat up in his bed. "I'm feeling better than yesterday, Patel Dada."

"What are the doctors saying, Anil?" He turned to Param's father.

"He has suffered a concussion, but he will recover in a week or two. I believe he goes home today." His father answered.

"But we will take him to our house," his mother answered.

"Mom, I can go home—"

"No." And that was that. He didn't have the energy to argue with her.

"I need to see Rani," he said.

"I know about the whole faking thing," Patel Dada said.

"Yes. I'm sorry we lied to you, it's just that... Milan—"

Patel Dada put his hand up to stop him. "Are you canceling the wedding?"

Param stared at the old man for a moment. His parents and brothers watched him, waiting for the answer. He summoned his strength. "Yes, Patel Dada, we are canceling. I will not be getting married for real, so the trust will not be able to be opened."

Silence filled the room. Param just wanted everyone to leave so he could be free to have a minor breakdown. He let down his little brother and lost the love of his life all in one blow.

"Do you remember, beta, when you asked me what would happen to the money if the three of you never married?" Patel Dada asked him.

Param nodded.

"Your grandfather loved your grandmother dearly. You didn't really know her, because she died when you were toddlers. But he had always wanted that for the three of you." Patel Dada paced the floor. "But he was no fool. He knew there might be a situation in which one or more of you never married for any number of reasons. He certainly did not want any of you to enter into a marriage solely to get this money. So he asked me to observe. And that is what I did." Patel Dada came and sat on the edge of Param's bed. "What I saw is what your family already knows. You and Rani love each other. Whether you are able to get married, I will leave up to you." He stood and looked at Milan, then their father. "Anil, as far as I am concerned, the requirements of the trust have been fulfilled. I will unlock it and make the funds available to these boys equally, to do with whatever they please."

He turned and looked at Param. "So, if you marry Rani, it can be because you love each other, and only that."

Chapter Forty

Rani left Param's room just after the 5:00 a.m. vitals check. He was looking better, and the nurses were taking great care of him. And he was right. If they weren't going to be together, they needed to learn to be apart.

She left so she would not be there when his parents arrived with chai and snacks to feed an army.

She went home. She took a long, hot shower and then she set an alarm and she crawled into her bed and closed her eyes. She drifted from sleep to awake to sleep, and in that in-between time, she caught the comforting aroma of chai. And not just any chai, but her mom's chai, and she drifted off to sleep.

The alarm went off too soon, but she had to be at the clinic today for a few hours. She quickly changed and gathered her things.

"Hey." Sona was in the kitchen on her laptop. "Did you hear?"

"Hear what?" Rani said as she grabbed her coat.

"Patel Dada is releasing the money whether you and Param get married or not."

So now Param had no reason to marry her, and she did not need to marry him. Her heart sank a little. Huh. "That's fabulous."

"Aren't you eating?" Sona asked

"No."

"Well, I'm sure Auntie took a ton of food to the hospital. You can just eat there," Sona said.

"I'm not going to the hospital. I have to be at the clinic." Rani started to leave.

"Wait, you're not going to see him?" Sona was a bit more than a little judgy in that moment.

"What? I was there all night." Rani changed her mind and looked for a granola bar or something.

"Yeah, but it's after noon now and he's your best friend." Sona mumbled something she couldn't hear.

Just as well. Rani could guess what she was saying.

"Well, things change."

"What the hell does that mean?"

"I gotta go." Rani left

She was busy at the clinic, thank goodness, so she didn't have to think about Param at all. But that did not stop her brain from drifting to thoughts of him anyway. Not to mention her heart aching a bit as well. It was not pleasant.

She walked into an exam room and found Malini Sharma in there with her mother.

"Hey, Malini. How are you?"

"What are you doing here, Dr. Rani?" the little girl asked.

"I'm seeing patients."

"No, I mean why are you here and not with Mr. Sheth at the hospital"

"You heard about that?" Rani asked.

"Of course."

"The school sent out an email to the parents. So we could talk to the children," her mother explained.

"So…why aren't you with him? He's your best friend and you're supposed to get married. Although, you may have to postpone the date since he has a concussion."

"We aren't getting married anymore," Rani told her, and sadness fell over her.

"What?" Malini stood up.

"We broke up," Rani explained.

"Then un-break up." Malini said this like it was obvious and so easy.

"It's complicated, Malini."

"Yeah, that's what he said. But you just need to talk to each other. That's what Amy and I do. And my boyfriend, Trevor."

"I'll keep that in mind. And did you say Trevor was your boyfriend? When did that happen?" Rani sat down next to Malini.

"It happened last week. Didn't Mr. Sheth tell you?" Her eyes were wide with disbelief.

"No. I'm afraid Mr. Sheth and I haven't talked in a while," Rani told her sadly.

"Don't waste time," Malini said. "Trevor said he liked me for a long time, but I had a crush on…someone else, so I didn't notice. Time was wasted."

Rani stared at this sweet young girl. Then she hugged her. "You're a pretty smart girl."

Rani finished her shift and went home without going

to see Param She had started walking over, then thought better of it and walked to her car. She sat in her car for a full five minutes wondering how he was. Her phone dinged and it was a text from Veena Auntie, updating them all. Param was being discharged soon but would be going to his parents' house for the night so he wouldn't be alone.

There. He was fine. Well taken care of. He did not need her.

Rani drove up to her house, but there were no cars in front and the house looked dark. She pulled out of the driveway and swung around to Param's house. Everyone's car was there.

She drove past. She did not need to be there to cancel her wedding. They could all handle that.

She drove around, not really paying attention to where she was going, and found herself in front of her masi's house.

She and her sisters used to spend a week here every summer when they were growing up, with Shreya Masi and Tanmay Masa. But they didn't go together. They each got a week alone at masi's. It was something they had all looked forward to. Masi and Masa didn't have any children of their own, so they adored spending that special time with each girl.

After her mother died, they didn't go Shreya Masi's for two summers. Rani hadn't understood why, and she had missed that time with her aunt. Then one day, Shreya Masi showed up at the house. She and her father had a conversation, and then asked who wanted to go first to masi's house.

Rani sat in the driveway as the winter sun set. Masi's

house was a small rancher, the lights were on. She parked the car and rang the bell.

Shreya Masi opened the door, seeming for all the world completely unsurprised to see her. Masi was the younger sister, but right now, she looked exactly like Rani's mom.

"Rani," she said, and she stepped aside to let her in.

Rani stepped inside the house, and the familiar scents of chai and cooking spices and her mom's perfume enveloped her. She hugged Shreya Masi and burst into tears.

The arms that surrounded her and the voice that comforted her were so like her mom that Rani melted into that embrace and sobbed.

When she quieted, Masi led her into the small kitchen where they sat down at the small island. Masi wiped away her tears and presented Rani with a cup of chai.

Rani blew her nose and settled, allowing the aromas of cinnamon, clove and cardamom to comfort her. Masi sipped her chai in the chair next to her.

"Why did you not come get us when Mom died?" Rani asked.

Masi inhaled and sipped her chai, and looked at Rani with love, tinged with sadness. "Because you were hers, you were part of her, and it was too hard to see you and know she was gone. She was all I had left. My strong big sister. I couldn't bear it." Masi ran her hand over Rani's hair like she had when Rani was a child. "I was scared and I hurt you girls, and your father and I regret it every day."

"What made you decide to come get us again?"

"Well, first, because I missed the heck out of you three. I also knew Deepti Ben would have so angry at me for not being there for her children." She looked down at her chai and then took a sip. "But mostly because your mother was the strongest person I knew. She did the things that scared her no matter what. You heard her friends at your house. My sister was so full of life. She didn't shy away from anything, no matter if she was afraid or sad. She put herself out there, damn the consequences. I came to get you because I wanted to be more like her. I didn't want to be afraid. I was still alive and she wasn't. She never wasted one second of her time on earth—who was I to waste the time I had been given?"

Masi squeezed Rani's arm and returned to her chai. Rani sipped hers in silence.

"They are canceling my wedding," she said finally.

"I heard," Masi replied quietly.

"I love him," Rani said the words softly, testing them out.

Masi nodded. "I know you do." She smirked a little. "Everyone knows you do. Everyone but him."

Rani finished her chai as they sat in silence a bit longer.

"Look at Aisha and Milan. They have no guarantees. But they are living," Masi noted. "You need to make a choice. You can choose to live your life or you can choose to exist in your life." She looked Rani in the eye and Rani glimpsed her mother again, in the set of her mouth, the fierceness in her eyes. "Living requires risk and you will get hurt. Existing is safe." Masi stood to clear the mugs. "The choice is yours."

Chapter Forty-One

Param needed to break out of his room. He needed to see Rani. He couldn't leave things the way they were.

The problem was that the whole family was gathered downstairs in the process of canceling the wedding. There was no getting past them. Also, he had no idea where she was.

He sat up in bed and sent out a text. He had one ally downstairs.

Ten minutes later, his door opened and instead of Aisha, his brothers entered the room.

"I wanted to talk to Aisha." His irritation was more from the small hammers in his head than anything else.

"Yes. She told us you texted," Milan said as they sat down on his bed. "She said you want to make a break for it."

Param closed his eyes. "You know I spent a lot of time wondering how many women could walk away from me in a lifetime." he said out loud. He didn't need to open his eyes to know his brothers were looking at each other. He opened his eyes and looked at them. "When you get left at the mandap, you start to feel... less than."

"That was Sangeeta's issue—not yours," Nishant said.

"I understand that—now. But I didn't see it coming, did I?" He glanced away for a moment. "But Rani was—is—my best friend. No matter what happened between us, she never made me feel like less. Even after Sangeeta, Rani always made me feel like I was more than enough." He paused. He didn't need to be the smartest like Nishant, or the most talented like Milan. Rani loved him for him.

And she did love him, whether she wanted to act on it or not.

Their story was not over.

"I need to find her," he said.

"You're supposed to be resting." Nishant smirked at him.

"Rani is not walking away from me that easily. Are you going to help me?" His head pounded lightly.

His brothers stood and looked at each other before they left his room.

What the—? Some brothers. Guess he was on his own. He stood and started trying to dress without falling over.

"Whoa. Whoa. What are you doing?" Nishant and Milan were back. Param collapsed on his bed.

"Getting dressed. I'm not going to see her in my pajamas." He had on jeans. "She likes that blue long sleeve shirt thing." He waved at his closet.

Nishant tossed him the shirt. Milan handed him his shoes and jacket.

"Where is she?" Milan asked.

"No idea," said Param.

"I know where she is." Sona's voice came from the door. "So I'm coming too."

He got down the stairs with little help and was halfway to the mudroom when his mother called out, "Take the ring with you, Param."

They got in Sona's car and drove the hour to Shreya Masi's house. Param was feeling better by the time they got there, so he got out of the car and rang the bell.

Shreya Masi answered the door and a huge grin fell over her face. "You missed her, Param. She left half an hour ago."

"Where did she go?"

"I'm sorry, beta. She didn't say."

Param returned to the car. "She was here, but she just left. Where would she go from here?"

Sona laughed. "She's looking for you."

Param laughed with her. "She's at my parents' house."

Rani left her masi's house with a new sense of urgency. She needed to find Param. She needed to talk to him. She needed to tell him.

She drove up to his parents' house and nearly ran into the house to find him. Now that she had decided what she wanted to say, she wanted to say it right away. Her heart raced as she entered the mudroom and heard the laughter coming from the kitchen. Everyone was here. It didn't matter.

Rani was her mother's daughter. She was done being afraid. She bounded into the kitchen.

"Hey!" she said with laughter in her voice.

Everyone turned to look at her and the kitchen fell silent. Even Veer didn't make a sound.

"Um, hi. Look, I know you all know that Param and I were faking, but we meant well."

No one spoke for another beat. Until Karina spoke up. "What are you doing here?"

"I…uh…came to see Param." Panic swooped in. "Why? Isn't he here?"

"No. He's—"

"Did he have to go back to the hospital?" She glanced around. "Is that where Nishant and Milan are? Did they take him to the hospital?" She started to turn to go back to the mudroom for her shoes and jacket. "You could have texted me that he was going." She shot out at Karina, more than a little panic in her voice. What if she had waited too long? What if something happened and it was too late?

"I'm not in the hospital." Param's voice came from behind her, deep and smooth. A little strained, but his voice undeniably.

She turned around to find him dressed in jeans and the long sleeve T-shirt she really liked. He hadn't shaved in a day or so, his hair was tousled and he was as handsome as ever.

"You are a very hard woman to track down." He grinned at her.

"Right back at you," she said.

"Were you looking for me?"

She flushed, suddenly aware that there was a rapt audience. She bit her bottom lip and met his eyes. The amusement and love she found there wrapped her in a bubble in which only she and Param existed.

"I was." She lifted her chin. "Looking for you. And

look. Here you are." She looked behind him at Sona and his brothers. "Where were you?"

He stepped closer to her, that fantastic smile on his face. "Looking for you."

"Okay," Karina spoke up. "Let's go, family. Time to give them some privacy and go to the movies or something. Leave them here or we may never have this wedding."

The entire family cleared out in what felt like less than thirty seconds. Rani found herself alone with Param. He walked over to the island and patted it with his good hand. She hopped up onto her spot, and Param leaned against the island right next to her. She inhaled his familiar scent and was instantly calmed.

"So. Why were you looking for me?" he asked, but he had a knowing smile on his face.

"You first." How could he possibly know what she was going to say? "Why were you looking for me?"

"Because I am in love with you, Rani. And I know that you love me, and that you're afraid. I wanted to tell you that I will always be here. That I'll wait for you to realize that I am the one for you. Because you, Rani Mistry, you are the only one for me. All this time, I wanted to be loved for who I was, and all this time, you were right here, doing just that."

Rani's heart pounded in her chest and every cell in her body danced with joy. She could not have kept the smile from her face if she had tried.

He leaned even closer, his breath tickling her ear. "Your turn."

She met his eyes. Deep brown, familiar, loving eyes. "I wanted to tell you that I love you, too. That you are everything I've ever wanted or needed and it took almost losing you—" her voice cracked "—for me to see it. Loving you, being with you, is more than worth the risk of losing you." She paused and bumped his shoulder. "And what you said about not wanting to be friends with me?"

"Yes?"

"I don't want to be friends with you either."

"No?" He mock furrowed his brow and shook his head.

"No." She grinned wickedly. "I mean, we could be friends, but then I wouldn't be able to do this." She closed the small gap between them, placing her lips gently against his. He responded immediately, opening her mouth and deepening their kiss like he was parched and she was water.

They pulled apart for breath. "I agree," he whispered. "Being friends won't work."

He produced a small box from somewhere and opened it. "Thing is, that night we sat right here, sharing our lives like we always do, I never actually proposed."

The ring was the most beautiful she had ever seen.

"Rani Mistry. You are my best friend and I have fallen in love with you. It may never be the same as it was, Rani, but I promise to do my best to make it better. I don't even know when I started falling in love with you. It might even have been the day we met when we were ten years old. All I know is that sometime during the past twenty years, I realized not only that I couldn't be without you, but that I would choose to be with you every day for the rest of my life."

Rani bit her bottom lip and took the ring from the box. "I choose…" Tears burned at her eyes as she looked up at him. She slipped the ring on her finger. "I choose to love you, too. I choose the unknown with you, over the known without you, any day."

Param Sheth, her very best friend in the whole world, leaned in again and kissed her senseless. "Marry me," he said, his voice thick and gravelly. "Marry me and we'll tackle all the unknown together."

"Yes." Rani managed between kisses. She took his face in her hands and looked him in the eye. "Yes. Yes. Yes."

She leaned in to continue making out with her husband-to-be when Milan's voice came from the kitchen entrance.

"She said yes, people. We have a wedding to plan!"

A cheer erupted from their families, who clearly had a thing or two to learn about the meaning of privacy.

Epilogue

Three days later, they had finished the Ganesha Puja and it was their wedding day. They were getting married in Rani's home, tent and all.

Param was already seated in the mandap for the groom's ceremonies. Rani was upstairs in her parents' bedroom having the finishing touches put on her as she waited to be called downstairs.

"Look at me," Aisha said.

Rani stood and faced Aisha as her future sister-in-law drew a critical eye over her lengha.

"Perfect," she confirmed, turning her gaze to Rani's face. She narrowed her eyes. "More lip gloss though."

Pankthi rolled her eyes. "She has plenty of gloss. She needs more eyeliner."

Just then Karina entered and looked at her sister. "My baby sister." Tears welled in her eyes as took Rani in. "Mom would be—well, you know." She swallowed her tears. "Her makeup is fine, but I could use a hand."

Karina had been down prepping food, and her dupatta was falling off her shoulder.

Pankthi stood to help her just as Sona entered from taking pictures of Param.

She smirked at Rani. "That man looks amazing."

"Oh. Let me see the pics," Rani said.

"No way." Sona held her camera out of her reach. "You'll see when you see."

Rani's heart was full. She had everyone she loved under this roof, and in a little bit, she would be married— for real this time—to her best friend.

Karina puttered around the room, acting so much like their mother that Rani cried while she laughed. In an instant, all three girls were hugging her.

Aisha got a text. "It's time."

Rani stood and took a deep breath. It was all she could do to not run down the stairs and into Param's arms. Once she had decided to marry him, she wanted to just marry him already.

Pankthi walked first, then Aisha, then Sona and lastly, Karina and Veer.

Rani walked behind her nephew, who had decided to greet each and every guest who stood along the aisle.

Both sides.

She removed her shoes and stepped into the mandap facing the antarpat. Milan and Nishant grinned at her before dropping the white cloth to reveal Param standing on the other side, holding a flower haar in his good hand.

His face glowed and he shook his head at whatever nonsense Nishant had just whispered to him. She couldn't take her eyes off of him. She caught her father's eye and he beamed with joy. They all missed her mother, but the very wedding itself was a celebration of everything she was. So they had agreed that no tears would be shed today.

Param did not want to take his eyes away from Rani's. He knew her smile, her face, those eyes. But the way she looked at him today, it was as if no one else existed for her in that moment but him. It was just the two of them ready to solidify promises they had made to each other over the course of their lifetime.

Aisha handed her a flower garland similar to the one he held. Rani held out the haar at the instruction of the priest. She raised her hands and Param bent down and she placed the haar over his head to loud cheering. Param then placed his haar over her head, and the dhol hit a beat while everyone cheered and tossed flower petals.

They did their four turns around the sacred fire, made their seven vows, played all the games. Param's wallet was lighter after paying Karina and Sona to get his shoes back.

He glanced at Rani, who laughing with Milan, and his heart thudded again in his chest. He walked over and took her hand, leading her to the sofa. He sat in the corner, bringing her close to him. His brothers and their wives joined them, along with Uncle, his parents and Rani's sisters.

"What's up?" She looked at him.

He shrugged. "Patel Dada requested our presence. All of us."

With that, Patel Dada entered the family room and stood.

"Congratulations to the new couple." He tipped his head to them, his face light and happy. "It is an auspicious day, so I have one last order of business." He paused. "Your grandfather's trust." He walked around and handed each brother, and each wife an envelope. "Divided exactly as he requested. Amongst all the children." He nodded. "Use it wisely."

Rani looked at Param, and they both stood and walked over to Patel Dada. She gave him a big hug. "Don't be a stranger, especially now since you're a One Republic fan."

"Thank you, beti." He nodded at the room and left.

Then Param's wife—he would never tire of referring to her that way—walked over to Milan and handed him her envelope. Param followed behind her and did the same. Nishant and Pankthi were right behind them. Surgery was scheduled for two weeks. Milan and Aisha were leaving two days after the wedding.

Milan was speechless. Aisha teared up. "You didn't even open them."

"Don't need to," Param said, taking his seat again. Rani curled up next to him, his arm draped over her shoulder. He held her tight. She turned to look at him and kissed her. "I have everything I need, right here."

* * * * *